Unfamiliared

J E HANNAFORD

PB ISBN: 978-1-7385167-4-2

EB ISBN: 978-1-7385167-5-9

Edited by Diana James.

This one is for Andrew.
Without whom, I would never have finished my first book

Chapter One

I reached for Archie's small, furry body, desperate to get hold of him, to pull him back to safety, but he was beyond reach. My fingers closed around air as the portal decorated my wrist with feathers of frost. The beautiful crystals entwined as they extended up my arm and into my chest. Each breath ripped warmth from my lungs and left me shaking with lancing agony where the frost grew.

With a pop, the portal closed, and I doubled over in shock as the magic withdrew from my body. Tingling pain ran down my arm as the frost melted, leaving a faint trace of silvery patterns on my arm. Darkness filled the hole where once Archie had been, then flowed onward into the void where my magic had burned, inaccessible without his presence. My power was gone – along with both my familiar and every other familiar in Witchgorn.

Milla and I had been entrusted with their care this afternoon. The familiars worked hard, and every few days we took it in turns to supervise their rest time, a frolic in the fields, while the protectorate did those quick tasks it's easier to do without being stared at; it should have been relaxing.

I sat in a crumpled heap and tried to rub warmth back into my arm, desperately hoping that the lack of magic was a temporary effect of the portal. My optimism was shattered within moments when a cry of shock came from Gail's home. Her door flew open as she ran into the street.

'Where are they?' she called.

'Gone. A portal took them.' How stupid did that sound? I winced.

'Then you'd better get to Pigs Might Fly, and fast.' Gail hitched up her skirts and ran toward our meeting house.

I rose reluctantly. It was time to face the consequences – not that it was *all* my fault. Someone should have been with me. Who leaves the newest member of the village protectorate alone in charge of all the familiars? Milla told me she'd only be a minute, but she'd been gone ages.

My skirt was crumpled and, as I had done many times in the last few months, I wished I could just wear the clothes I used to. But this was my new life, and the skirt came with it, like some sort of ancient uniform. I dusted down my clothes and set off toward where I hoped to find Pigs Might Fly.

The others would figure it out soon enough. Judging by the way I felt, they already knew. The scent of food that had drifted from the portal was just too much, and not one familiar would listen to me. They'd leapt through willingly – even Archie. So much for them being intelligent.

I took small comfort from the surety that I'd know if something bad had happened to him. The time he'd stood on a sharp splinter, I'd felt his pain across the entire village. He was alive, whatever or whoever had lured him through the portal, but so far away, I couldn't access my magic.

I swallowed the cold lump of fear and tried not to vomit in

the hedge. Was it the lack of magic making me feel sick, or the fact that I was going to have to confess I'd lost all our familiars into an unknown plane with no idea how to get them back?

The villagers of our idyllic village of Witchgorn were about to discover what life without magical protection was truly like, what the villages of the unhidden lands were like, those under the rule of Seastone Keep.

My legs grew leaden with each step towards Pigs Might Fly. I gritted my teeth, focused on its last known location and determined to get aboard before it was lost to me. I could always borrow a magic mask from a non-magicker, but I needed to believe that there was some remnant of power left – enough to locate a wandering coffee house.

I rounded the wall of the pub to see the majority of the village protectorate wandering around the field with their arms outstretched as they tried to locate a, now invisible to us, cafe with a tendency to walk wherever it wanted.

A small crowd of residents had gathered to spectate, entirely unaware of what the scenario meant for them.

I reached for the mask dangling from the nearest belt. Aran was never the most observant of fellows and would probably think he'd dropped it. I'd lost count of how many new ones we'd made him. I slipped the mask on under my hood, grateful that the village protectorate allowed the villagers access to the lower floor of the coffeehouse. Pigs Might Fly snapped into view as soon as the mask was in place, so I strolled up to the door, catching the steps as the coffee house started to lift.

Maybe all the patting of its walls had unsettled it. Certain the others would soon follow, I climbed the stairs to the second floor and sank to my spot in our circle to await my fate.

Footsteps pounded the floorboards as I studied the grain of the wood in front of my seat. The whirling knot midway along the plank was unsettlingly like the swirls of the closing portal.

Gail entered, and the other five women followed close on her heels, each with a mask dangling from their hand. The room was subdued, less alive without our familiars. Even Pigs Might Fly sank back down again, after gentle reassurance from Satu, instead of moving to a new spot as it usually did when disturbed.

Cari Elphick strode in last. The door closed behind her with a soft click.

'No one leaves this room until I have an explanation.' Her gaze swept the room, landing on Milla before settling on me. 'Eva Eclipse and Milla Russet, where are the familiars?'

Her voice was dangerously low, and given that I'd seen her persuade a turtle to dance only yesterday, I knew she was more than capable of puppeteering me normally. Turtles are incredibly hard to coax into anything against their will. But Cari didn't have her familiar – and without Ralph to channel her magic, she couldn't make a grain of sand dance. She was just an old woman. Or at least that's what I tried to tell myself as she tapped her foot impatiently.

'I wasn't there,' Milla blurted. 'I told her to watch them while I took a quick nature break.'

The only nature break Milla had taken involved the dark-haired man with a gentle voice who'd been making cow-eyes at her over the fence for the last two days. I considered throwing her to the protectorate then and there, but keeping that secret close to my chest might help me in the long run.

'I was just—'

'Just?' Cari raised an eyebrow. *Just* is not a word I want to hear right now. Be concise, child.'

Child? I was older than half these women. I was just a late bloomer – well, magically anyway. I resisted the urge to point it out and tried to remain calm and factual.

'A portal opened up in the field where they were all playing.

Some sort of pipe music and delicious smells emanated from it. The familiars ran into it faster than I could catch them, as though drawn, or sucked in.'

'Were they sucked in?' Gail looked horrified, but Cari held her hand up to silence the murmurs rippling around the room.

'Their feet did leave the floor.' I cringed. 'I tried to catch them, really, I did. It was cold so very cold.' My arm hurt at the thought of that portal. I pulled my sleeve up to expose the frosted scar.

Satu leant toward me, studying my arm.

'They tested us early. I told you we should have reminded everyone about the testing.' She looked up at me. Her stern expression made me want to curl a little smaller. 'Did you get any sense of danger from Archie?'

The image of Dotty, Amy Marsh's familiar, levitating through the portal, her curly tail flicking her plump, porcine bottom with excitement, passed through my mind.

'They didn't appear scared.'

'Well, that's all great, then. The familiars are kidnapped, we are undone. We're the first protectorate to fail the test in years.' Amy squealed like a pig when she was upset. She and Dotty were well suited.

'We'll get them back. I just need to figure out which type of portal it was, then recast it, backwards, without my own familiar.' Cari sat in the centre of the circle. 'We all know they'll be back. No one can hold Sirathon for long. He'll fly back as soon as he can.'

Gail snorted. 'He's a duck, not a homing pigeon.'

'He'll be back.' Satu placed a reassuring hand on Gail's arm.

I stood awkwardly, unsure if I was dismissed or worse – about to be stripped of my place in the protectorate.

'So, we've failed. It doesn't mean they have to know they get them all, though, right? We can still host the Games?'

Milla had to be joking, surely. We were hosting my first inter-village Games as a competitor. I'd watched with amazement the few times they had been here in the past. Now my chance to actually compete had floated away through a portal with my wonderful, furry old boy.

I loved watching the lumbering golem that guarded our gates racing against others from villages in Two Chasms, the clouds dancing to the commands of magikers from here, and old Lola Silone winning the beanstalk growing contest.

Lola. She was retired; it was her place I'd taken.

'Dandelion wasn't in the field. Lola must still have him.' It was one familiar. One source of magic.

'Dandelion is so old that he can only feed Lola enough magic for a single spell each day before they both fall back asleep.' Gail snapped.

'That's one spell a day more than the rest of us,' Cari murmured. 'For now, we won't tell anyone what's happened. Milla and Eva, as you lost them, you will scour the village for replacements to our familiars and take them all to Lola's house.'

'We can't replace them,' Satu said. 'But letting the villagers believe that we still have familiars would help them – especially after that little display outside. If we consider this alongside the news from Berta Kimura, leader of the Sentraal protectorate, that someone has been causing trouble in a number of the southern villages, it might be a bigger problem than a prank. It's been small stuff, but causing a constant drain on their magic to keep fixing them. This is probably a pre-Games test, but we should keep our minds open. We can't risk looking weak enough that we are ripe for takeover.'

Both suggestions brought little comfort. Hanging on to my belief that I'd know if Archie was harmed, and not seeing panic on any of the other's faces, I stood up. In a village this small, where was I going to find six co-operative animals who also looked just like the originals? I opened my mouth to ask, but Cari's expression changed my mind in a hurry.

'We'll get right on it,' I said, and gestured for Milla to join me. She uncurled in that languid way that the young and beautiful must spend hours perfecting, and we left Pigs Might Fly in silence.

Chapter Two

'Who shall we start with?' Milla asked once we were across the field and away from earshot of anyone. 'I really don't think this is going to work!' She pouted her plump lips and tossed long golden curls over her shoulder before hitching up the very unfashionable skirts we wore and stomping up the road.

'Farmer Rob Tomkin has a few pigs. We could try to find one that looks enough like Dotty there? Aren't his all spotted too?'

Milla changed direction, taking a narrow path through the field and away from the village.

'You can't just run off and find that cow-eyed man again,' I called. 'That's what got us in this situation in the first place. You shouldn't have left me.' I wasn't magically weak, but having started using it so late, my range of abilities was still developing. Milla was experienced. If she'd been there, she'd probably have known about this test and been able to affect the portal.

She had the grace to look embarrassed, the red flush rising in her cheeks as she turned to me.

'We'll do the easy ones last. First, we need to catch a wild duck from the pond for Gail. Stop worrying. They're all still alive – we'd feel it otherwise, so it's probably just the test.'

I buried my fear a little. She was right – and about the duck too. Sirathon would be the hardest familiar to replace.

No one really understands how the whole *familiar* thing works. It's not like you just awake one day with a magical animal companion sleeping alongside you. Well, most people don't. In my case, I did, but that was more a case of me blooming so late that my familiar had spent his youth being treated as any stray pet taken into a home and spoilt would. He was walked on a lead – something he'd later informed me in no uncertain terms was the highest level of indignity I'd unwittingly bestowed on him. The other familiars had teased him that he'd picked wrong all those years ago. But he'd stuck by me, and the thought of replacing him – even outwardly – churned my guts like a spoiled glass of milk. He'd be back, somehow. I had to trust Cari on that.

I was snapped out of my thoughts by a splash near my right boot as Milla laid a restraining hand on my arm. A duck flapped away, and my boot filled with water. *Great.*

'Which one do you think looks most like Sirathon?' she asked as we looked at the pond full of ducks. Their green heads glinted, and curly feathers at their rear ends fluttered like small pennants.

'They all look the same to me.' I couldn't spot any difference between them. A duck was a duck, was a duck. 'How do you propose we catch one?'

'I thought you might know, what with you being more mature than me when you joined. You know, having to be self-sufficient and everything.'

I had been about to point out the closest duck, who appeared the least afraid – maybe suggest that offering some crumbs or food would entice them closer – but her dig at my age stopped me.

'I think we just need to wait until one has its back turned, then leap on it,' I said. 'I've seen people do that before.' It wasn't an untruth. I'd just left one tiny detail out …

'Well, as I'm younger, and probably more agile, I'll do it.'

Oh, she deserved this.

Milla hitched her skirts a little higher, tucking them into her waistband, and waded into the water. Ducks swam away from her as she closed on them … all, that is, aside from one drake, who had his head underwater, foraging. Milla targeted him. She crouched, and with a sudden leap into action, she pounced.

'Gotch—' Spluttering and duck-less, Milla landed face first in the water as the drake dived a little deeper and escaped her clutches. She stood up, soaked from head to toe, pond weed in her hair and her perfect makeup running in black rivers down her cheeks, and laughed.

'There's no way this is going to work.' She bent forward and sluiced her face with more water. 'Any other ideas?'

'Try it on land,' I offered. 'We could try to bribe them with bread or something, then sneak up on one.'

She squelched out from the pond. 'I'm not sneaking up on anything like this.' Milla wrung her skirts out and removed each shoe, pouring water from them while still giggling. 'When I was little, we'd spend hours at this pond. We all saw Gail with Sirathon, and so everyone hoped to catch their own magical duck. Now it seems I can't even catch one to be a fake familiar.' She put her feet back in the wet shoes. 'Aran tried the hardest to tame one. He was desperate to be chosen.'

'In Witchgorn? Why didn't he move to Sentraal? He'd have stood a chance there.' The familiars in Witchgorn had only chosen women for years. In Sentraal, they were less picky, and all sorts of people were chosen as magic wielders.

Milla shrugged. 'He's nothing if not persistent.'

'Aran Burtle? The one who loses his mask at least once a week? Who walks around in a dream?' Persistent wasn't a word I associated with Aran.

'Yes. It's not his mask that gets lost, you know. He offers his to anyone who loses theirs. I cast a follow charm on one, once. He just handed it over when Rob had his eaten by the pigs.'

'Why doesn't he say that?'

She shrugged again. 'Dunno, but I do know that if anyone can catch us a duck, it's Aran.'

'No one is supposed to know.'

Milla rolled her eyes at me so far round that I thought she must have looked at the inside of her own skull. 'Eva Eclipse, are you telling me that you wouldn't recognise our familiars in a lineup of pigs, goats, sheep, and dogs? Do you seriously think that someone who has spent his life watching and hoping, even more intently since you bloomed so late, isn't going to know that we swapped animals?'

She was right. With the best will in the world, Cari's idea would fail. We could only hope that persuading the villagers to help would give the illusion to whoever was watching that we still had our familiars for long enough to get them back.

Aran sat in the field, watching people enter and leave the coffeehouse. Up three steps, vanish. Reappear. Down three steps to the grass. He patted at his belt, where I'd stolen his mask earlier, and I felt a small pang of shame.

'I found this – is it yours?' I offered him his own mask, and he looked up at me, his eyes narrowing briefly, before the glazed smile replaced it.

'Aran, we need your help.' Milla sat next to him, with rivulets of water draining from her.

'You should take those off before you swim,' he said. 'Did you lose your sense along with your familiars?'

'No! I mean, I have no idea what you mean,' Milla replied, once again blushing. She couldn't lie for her life.

'Milla, you never go anywhere without Fern. Not ever. And her ...' He cocked his head at me. 'Archie is at her heels with every step she takes. Always the same with newer magikers.'

'Do you think anyone else has noticed?' Milla whispered.

'Probably. None of us are as ignorant of what you all get up to as you'd like to think.'

'I agree with him,' I said. 'This isn't going to work. The second someone asks for the golem to be repositioned so a cart can get past, it's all over. Or, what about when old Elsie asks for that anti-ageing spell on her toes again?'

'It has to work,' Milla hissed. 'If any of the other villages find out we're defenceless, it might not be the Games they come for. It might be the whole village.'

'I hate to be the one stating the obvious, but surely the person who cast that portal knows full well that we're now minus our familiars.' I watched a child trip over what I presumed was Pigs Might Fly's foot.

'All the more reason to pretend. So, one group of people knows – a rogue group of magikers trying to find a base, or one village, but no one else does,' Aran offered. 'I've spent my life watching you all make sparks dance on your fingers and teaching turtles to dance. The Games are due here in the next few weeks, and whatever happens, we have to take part. Let me help.'

'Can you catch a duck?' Milla asked hopefully.

'I can, and Rob Tomkin owes me a favour. He has a sow a

lot like Dotty. If Elsie Bucket wants her feet to look young, she will paint in the missing spots where I ask her to.'

'That's two down, just four more to find.' I laid back in the grass, watching the clouds scurrying overhead, changing shapes as they passed. Grey, heavy clouds, ready to douse us in a torrent of rain, followed behind.

'We'd better get moving,' I said, 'before we're all as wet as Milla. Aran, take the duck and pig to the coffeehouse. We'll meet you there.'

'That leaves us with a goat, a rabbit, a small grey dog, and most tricky of all, a magpie,' Milla said. 'Let's start with the goat.'

I got to my feet and offered her a hand up. Wet clothes that heavy were hard to move in.

Chapter Three

A goat. We needed a brown goat with horns and a tufty tail that looked like Jerry. All our familiars were of local origin, so I had to hope that there would be one we could commandeer which would at least cooperate a *little*.

I'd never met a goat that liked me. Even when I used to babysit for the Flutterbarks as a teenager, I used to get chased through the front door, and one of the goats would camp on the doorstep, refusing to let me out until the parents came back. Getting hold of one was not something I was looking forward to. Maybe Milla would be more goat-friend than I was.

Jerry was every bit as belligerent as any goat I'd ever met. He was the only familiar that Pigs Might Fly had ever thrown out. I hadn't figured out I was a magiker at that point, and was enjoying a coffee when the stairs flattened into a slide, and the goat whizzed straight past us and out the door before Pigs Might Fly stood up and walked off.

Maybe the goat we found wouldn't have to be much different from the ones I'd met in the past after all.

'The Flutterbarks have goats.' Milla interrupted my pondering as we reached the well in the centre of town.

'Mmhm. So does Royce Worthy up in the hut by the woods.' Royce was kind. Maybe his animals would be kind too.

'That's a good idea. He has a whole collection ... pack ... what are a group of goats called?'

We turned toward the woods, apparently both in agreement that it was worth trying Royce before the demon goats of the Flutterbarks. 'What about a hustle of goats?' I offered.

Milla nodded. 'A horn – oh, how about a butt-load!'

This was definitely a side of Milla I could grow to like. The grass still held a lot of water in its depths as we waded across the field. It would have been drier to walk around the path, but Milla was already wet through, and my boots may as well both squelch at this point.

The rickety cottage sat on the edge of the woods, a big oak tree hung low over its eaves, and the house's gutters were filled with leaves and acorns from past years. Blue paint peeled from the door in strips, and I couldn't help but think that the bare wood patches were a goat horn-like distance apart. The windows were dusty, and if you didn't know better, the building looked abandoned. Milla looked at me, then down at her soggy clothes. 'Have you ever been in?' she asked.

I shook my head. 'Not even when we were kids. I knew him, but we weren't close. His family has always lived here. He used to walk back from school on his own since his parents were always busy with the animals.

Milla nodded. 'I can hear goats somewhere in the woods.' She pointed to the thickening branches where light struggled through, and I listened hard. There were definitely animal noises back there.

'I'll knock.' I stepped up to the door and gave it three sharp raps before retreating a step. No one likes to open a door and be nose-to-nose with a visitor.

The scrabbling of small feet and a whining proceeded the clicks of a few bolts and a gentle voice saying, 'Back, boy. I can't let them in if you stop me opening the door. That's a good lad.' The door cracked open and a bespectacled eye peered through the crack, along with a small wet nose at about shin height. 'Yes, can I help you?'

His glasses were so smeared, I couldn't believe that he could see through them.

'Hi, it's Eva.' I waved, feeling stupid seconds later. Of course he knew who I was. 'We need to borrow a goat, please. One that looks as much like Jerry as possible.'

'Why would you want another Jerry?'

He opened the door a little wider, and his mud-coated trousers – to the calf where he must have removed his boots – were every bit as filthy as his glasses. His striped shirt was reminiscent of the front door, and he ran a hand through his thatch of blonde hair. Some things didn't change.

'One Jerry is all the village needs.'

'Exactly,' Milla chimed in, peering out from behind me. 'Hi, Royce. We've accidentally – and temporarily – lost Jerry. But it's really important that outsiders don't know that. So we need a spare goat to pretend to be Jerry while we try to get the real one back.'

Royce opened the door fully. 'What absolute nutter would want to take Jerry?' His eyebrows had shot up past his hair line, and the small grey and brown dog at his feet looked every bit as confused.

'Someone trying to sabotage our hosting of the Games,' I replied. 'Milla, you weren't supposed to tell *everyone*!'

'I know. But if this is going to work, we need help from the actual animal's handlers. Does Archie listen to anyone but you?

No one will notice if I find a replacement rabbit – you all think Fern just sits and eats grass all day. Don't look at me like that, Eva. I know you do. But a goat? A pig, even a dog ... It's not going to work without help.'

'You've lost all those too?' Royce's mouth hung open. 'I can't imagine losing Doug.' He bent down to pat his dog's head, then he looked back up while he scratched the dog's ears. 'Tell me you still have the magpie?'

I shook my head.

'The duck?'

Milla shook hers.

'The cat?'

'We still have the cat,' I said slowly.

'Anyone else?'

I grimaced. 'No, can you lend us a goat? We really do need to pretend we still have a goat.'

'So ...' He stood up, removed his glasses, and cleaned them on his even grimier shirt. 'We have no magic to defend the town right now aside from an ancient cat and even older woman.'

'That's right.'

'How will you compete in the Games?'

It wasn't the question I'd expected. Fear, or worry maybe. Concern for the village's wellbeing, probably. It must have shown on my face.

'Look, I know I'm a bit out of town here, but the Games work like a show of strength, right? A test of which villages are well defended from each other and outside observers. Didn't Raventor try to take control of Mistead a few years back when Mistead did poorly at the Games? And I remember clear as day when Nevsern got taken over by Seastone Keep after they hosted the games. If you don't look like a working protectorate, then we're in trouble.' He reached to his left and grabbed a coat from somewhere, then stuffed his arms in. He stepped into his boots and whistled to Doug. The small grey-brown dog trotted at his heel beautifully. I hoped Archie was okay. I missed his close warmth and comforting presence.

'Let's go call the goats in, see what we can do. You can borrow Doug when the Games begin if you haven't found Archie by then, but you still need to convince him to go with you. He likes sausages. You'll need to visit him every day with sausages, and probably walk him.'

It was better than the fish-bits Archie liked. I could cope with a pocket of sausages.

We didn't have far to go before our way was blocked by the fence. Royce picked up a metal pole and hit the upright a few times. The loud noise alerted the butt-load of goats, and they came running towards us, led by a grumpy-looking goat. It had a big patch across one eye just like Jerry, and the rest was a similar shade of brownish grey.

'That one?' I pointed at the lead animal.

'Is a female. Jerry's male. '

I looked at the rest of the animals. It was like a goat who's who with every conceivable size, shape and colour. Except that the one at the front was the closest in both ways.

'It's got to be that one.' I shrugged.

Royce reached for the grumpy-looking goat, who leant into him for a scratch.

'Look, I know you think that the colour is everything, but I promise you, people will notice if it's a female. Dusty isn't going to pass for Jerry, without, you know ... *bits*. You can't just magic that up, especially without magic.'

I tried to hold back a giggle at the ridiculousness of the idea brewing in my head. 'You're right, but, as you say, if the deception is to protect the entire village, then we can involve – *must* involve – the entire village, for it to work. I think we can make

Dusty into a boy with words in the right ear and a needle in the right hands.'

Milla stifled a giggle. 'You're going to sew her some *bits*?'

'Not me,' I replied. 'We should ask Larent.'

Royce almost choked on the air as I said it. But if he could sew a pretty purse, why not ugly, dangly bits?' Attaching them would be harder, but I figured we could fix that later.

'If it doesn't hurt her, then great. You might have problems hiding her udders, though.'

I bent down to study the underside of Dusty. I'd seen bigger. She kicked mud in my face. Bloody goats.

Royce pulled a halter from his pocket and handed me the rope. 'If you catch her, you can borrow her.'

The second she saw the halter, Dusty wheeled on her hindquarters and galloped off into the woods, the rest of the butt-load in tow. Royce chuckled. 'Don't worry, she's going to be about as cooperative as Jerry. Send Satu out herself. She's the one who has to make it stick. Can't expect a non-goat person to do a goat person's job. While you're at it, call a meeting – when I hear you've done that, we'll talk again. You can't do this without the rest of the village. It's time we paid you all back for the years of protection and support.'

He smiled, turned, and walked back to his house, closing the door behind him.

'Well, that went well,' Milla said. 'We only need a magpie and a rabbit now if Aran caught the duck. I really think I should get changed before we return to the others, though. Pigs Might Fly hates wet floors.'

Chapter Four

Milla's house was every bit as perfect as I'd expected. She ushered me in to a pristine room with pink sofas and frilly white cushions. A litter tray for Fern was decorated with a sparkly ribbon, and a plush rabbit house with sweet-scented hay sat in the corner. I walked carefully across the deep pile carpet, feeling water squeeze between my toes with every step, and perched on the edge of a seat while she ran into another room.

'I'll be back in a moment!'

As I waited, the kitchen door opened, and Milla's mother peered out. 'Is that you, darling? Oh, Mistress Eva. I didn't expect company.' She covered her face, which was perfectly pleasant, and fluttered her hands in dismay. 'What must you think of me, all untidy and no makeup.'

I shrugged and pointed at myself. 'I have none on either. It's okay.'

'But you never wear it. I have a ...'

I stood, squelched over to her, trying to ignore her look of horror, and gently removed her hands from her face. 'You can wear it if it makes you feel good, but don't rely on appearances to set your own self-worth. You're so kind and caring, and everyone knows you're the best baker in town.'

She took a deep breath, and I thought she was about to reply, but instead, she shook her head and retreated into the kitchen, leaving me alone in her immaculate sitting room.

'Sorry, this takes longer without magic,' Milla called. Couldn't she get dressed without magic? When she eventually rejoined me, her wonky eyeliner gave away what she'd been attempting to do.

'It looks great,' I lied.

'It doesn't, but if mum only sees me from a distance, she won't berate me for lowering my standards.' She pointed at the back door. 'We need a rabbit.' I tried not to look at the door, where I knew her mother hid. Did Milla do her makeup too?

I followed her out into a garden enclosed by a high fence. I'd always assumed that it was for privacy, but now I could see it was to keep animals in, not eyes out. Milla walked between a selection of almost identical rabbits until she found one that looked no different from any of the others and picked it up.

'You'll do, Fennel.' She tucked the rabbit into the crook of her arm. 'You can't have just one rabbit,' she offered as she passed back into the house. 'They get lonely.'

We headed back to Pigs Might Fly, or more correctly, to where we'd last seen it. Aran sat in the field with a pink pig and a duck. He was remarkably dry.

'Thought you might need help to find it,' he mumbled and passed us each an eye mask. He looked at the rabbit and our lack of anything else, but said nothing.

'Thank you,' I said. 'You should come in with us.'

'Someone has to,' he replied, and with masks in place, we

mounted the steps to Pigs Might Fly's door, shoving the pig through the doorway ahead of us. I tapped the nearest wall.

'Don't eject them – we need them,' I murmured. A window rattled, and the door started to re-open.

'We're going to need Satu's help, fast.' Milla ran up the stairs two at a time, while Aran and I tried to keep the door shut, but it was battering at us, and only determination – and the pig's own desperation to escape hindering the door with her sheer bulk – had stopped our eviction by the time Satu arrived in the room.

'That's quite enough,' she demanded. Pigs Might Fly bucked a little and half-heartedly tried to open the door again.

'I mean it.' Satu stood in the middle of the room, hands on her hips, scolding the building. Pigs Might Fly sank back down to rest and fluttered a window.

'Don't give me any cheek, now.' Satu took a deep breath and nodded in satisfaction before turning to me. 'Eva Eclipse, trouble seems to follow you everywhere today. I hope you two found a solution to hide our position from the villagers. She stopped mid-sentence as she noticed Aran. 'Why's he in here?'

I smoothed down my skirt, walked around the pig, and approached her.

'They already know. Well, some of them do, and we can't do this without them. We can't magic up a walking golem or a cure for old toes, and we can't pretend we still have our familiars. The village knows us. They know them. If you want the outside world to think everything is as it was, that we haven't failed the test, then we need their help. They need to pretend, too, in case it's a non-village group – in case someone is watching us and looking for weakness. We have every skill needed to survive in this village without magic, but we need to find a way to make it *look* like magic.'

Aran coughed. I turned to look at him as the others did. To

our amazement, he pulled a coin from behind Milla's ear, then made it appear and disappear numerous times in front of our eyes. It was amazing.

'Aran!' Milla gasped. 'You do have magic!'

He laughed. 'No, it's called sleight of hand. It's a trick used to delight children, but it fooled you – for a second.'

Satu snorted. 'Not me.'

Aran raised an eyebrow. 'I've seen you play cards in the Phoenix Feather often enough to know you can do it too.'

Satu nodded. 'Small sleight of hand is one thing, but moving an entire golem? Making clouds dance? The Games have wardens ... they have anti-cheating.'

I could see what Aran was getting at. 'But as hosts, we choose the wardens, and they're looking for magic, for interference from bystanders. They won't be looking for non-magical interventions.' I gestured at Aran. 'They won't notice tricks of slight.'

'Sleight of hand,' he muttered.

'Whatever it's called. Satu, Royce said you can borrow Dusty, but only if you catch her yourself and we hold a whole town meeting. We need to do it fast before we get observed and the first guests arrive.' I found myself touching the skin on my damaged arm. It was starting to harden and grow itchy.

Satu nodded slowly. 'Before we announce the chosen games for this year, we still have to choose them from the official list.'

Aran raised his hand. 'If you call a meeting, Mistress Satu, I think you'll find we all want to help. It does the village no good to appear defenceless, so we'll make it work. No magiker will be expecting us normal folk to help. As long as they get food from us, we're invisible.'

'Let me talk to Cari.' Satu turned back to the stairs with a last warning call to Pigs Might Fly. 'They *all* stay, including the pig.' The cafe rattled as Satu glided back up to the meeting room above.

I sat at one of the villagers' tables in the room. It was strange to be in here with the place so empty. 'Well, that went better than I expected. Pigs Might Fly, can I have a coffee?' The machine on the counter rumbled a little, and Milla rushed over to it.

'Stop! Satu feeds Pigs Might Fly daily. There's a limit to how much we can ask of it if we want it to look normal when the guests arrive. No coffee without magic.'

'Fine. Are there any cookies back there?'

'Not that I can see. Mum must not have dropped them off before the whole familiar-eating-portal thing.'

A loud flapping and fluttering of wings distracted us as we remembered Aran's presence and that of the duck.

'How *did* you catch it?' I couldn't see a spot of wetness anywhere on him.

'I asked nicely, approached from the front, and picked it up.' He shrugged. 'Ducks are easy when you have food smeared on your arm.'

'If they are easy, why is it flapping now?' Milla pointed at the struggling duck as it started to flap again.

'I swear you all lose your common sense when you gain magic. How long did you expect me to hold a duck for?' How long does Sirathon sit still? Or the magpie?'

He had a point. We had to find something to appease the duck. I joined Milla by the counter and rummaged through a few old tubs until I had a reasonably sized pile of biscuit crumbs. They were probably stale, but I didn't think the duck would mind.

The duck, it turned out, was quite happy with stale crumbs, and the pig was rather keen on them too. At least they were no longer trying to escape. Milla's rabbit had tucked into the crook of her arm, so calm it almost looked like a part of her. It might be no true familiar, but it would be the only one that might pass for one. I reached down automatically to stroke Archie. My heart hurt when my hand touched air. I had to believe he was okay.

Up above us, we heard raised voices, and Pigs Might Fly trembled a little as we waited.

<h1 style="text-align:center">Chapter Five</h1>

The sound of booted feet on the stairs alerted us to Satu's return, then another set, and another. I tried to focus on keeping the pig still. Aran had reclaimed the now-full duck, and Milla sat at her table, stroking Fennel.

It wasn't Satu who entered first, but Amy, who squealed at the pig, which squealed back at her.

'I can't work with that. Look at it! It's positively a farm animal.'

Satu rolled her eyes as she entered the room. 'Amy, this is your new familiar, so make peace with it. Until Dotty is back, *this* is now Dotty.'

Amy approached Dotty-The-Second with a frown and ran her hands along the pig's flanks. 'I could dye a little extra marking here, I suppose, and maybe a ribbon in her tail. Does she know any commands?'

Aran spluttered.

Amy rounded on him, her eyes flashing. 'You! You sit in sly silence, and now it turns out you've been watching us all the time?'

Aran gave her his slightly absent smile, and she paused. It was a good defence, and for a second, I was almost fooled, but I'd seen another side to him now. Amy stopped mid-stride.

'No, Mistress Amy. I'm sure someone with your pig wrangling skills can do it very well, though. Dotty was the best behaved pig I've ever seen.'

'*Is*. She'll be back.' She turned to study Dotty-The-Second. 'I suppose we all have to do our part.' She ran her hands over the pig and was rewarded with a grunt of pleasure when she scratched its ear. She reached into her pocket and pulled out a small object, offering it to Dotty-The-Second, who took it enthusiastically, then nudged Amy for more.

Amy looked up. 'Ahh ... I've got this now.' She grinned. Dotty-The-Second kept nosing at her pocket. 'So, you love cheese too, then?' We need to get you sorted out – and maybe on a harness, just for now. I think I have a spare ribbon somewhere at home. Satu, I'll be back for the meeting this afternoon.'

Satu nodded as Amy led the cheese-obsessed pig out the door with more nibbles.

'Aran, we agree to your suggestion, and to make things less chaotic, we will meet at the Phoenix Feather this evening. I'll take that, as Gail will stay here for the afternoon.' She reached for the duck.

The duck pecked her. She nipped its beak between her fingers. 'Enough of that.' With her other hand, she reached for the rest of the duck and tucked it tightly under her arm. 'Aran, go tell Royce that I'll be there shortly. Then let the village know about the meeting.'

'Will do, Mistress Satu.' He turned and left, closing the door carefully behind him.

'We're still missing a magpie and a dog.' Satu stared at me with the intensity she usually reserved for weak coffee.

'I can use Doug, Royce's dog, for the Games, but I'll have to walk him every day until then, otherwise he'll just keep running back to Royce.'

Satu shuffled the duck. 'I suppose that makes sense. Maybe one of the villagers has a bird trap we can use. Although, if any of our familiars can get back from wherever they've been taken, it will be Ralph.'

Taken. My poor Archie. He was elderly, although our familiars don't quite age as normal animals do, and he had a delicate stomach. If whoever had him wasn't feeding him right, they would be suffering in a cloud of noxious gas. I took a small measure of satisfaction that he would punish them in his own way. Archie was also patient, very patient. The problem was that we didn't have time for a cunning magpie and patient dog to mastermind an escape.

'Do you want me to ask around about the bird trap?'

Satu shook her head. 'Not straight away. Magpies are flighty but loyal, and so far, we have no sense that our familiars have been hurt.

'Go make yourselves respectable, and then you need to call on Lola Silone. You can be the one to explain that her retirement is over. Milla, can you persuade your mother to bake us some bribes for this afternoon?'

Milla winced. 'I'll try.'

'Good. Off you go then. I have a duck to take upstairs, a cafe to soothe, and a goat to catch.'

Lola Silone's house was small and cosy. Since she'd retired, Lola had turned her hand to gardening. I'm not saying it was magically enhanced, but there were flowers blooming in her garden entirely out of season with the rest of the village. Last winter, when everything had been iced and frozen, she had a cactus in full bloom on her doorstep. Lola might not be best pleased when I had to tell her Dandelion's magic was all we had and gardening was probably off limits. Dandelion was an elderly ginger cat who slept all the time and had just enough magic left for a single use per day.

I wove between lush tomato vines laden with scarlet treasure and ducked under a hanging basket of snow drops.

No, this was not going to be a pleasant surprise. I tapped on the door, and the brass door knocker opened its eyes. 'Too good to knock with me, Eva Eclipse?' it said.

'No, I just, well … There's been a bit of a small problem.' I caught myself. I was talking to the door. Lola had always found novel ways to integrate magic into her home. 'I need to speak to Lola.'

'She's asleep. Come back tomorrow.'

I sighed and placed my hand on the door handle, twisting it and pushing through anyway.

'Lola! Lola, Eva Eclipse is here. She won't go away,' the door knocker screamed in a whiny, metallic voice.

'Then let her in.' Lola's voice floated from the next room, so I walked toward it.

'Thank you for letting me in.' I bobbed a full-skirted curtsey to the sulking door knocker. It huffed and closed its eyes.

Dandelion stretched, then padded over to wind around my legs in greeting. It was hard to walk with the affection, but I accepted it gratefully.

Lola was far from asleep, seeing as she was deep in a book. I tried to peer at the cover, but she tucked a pressed leaf between the pages and rested it face down on a squat table next to her.

'You've not visited me since you took my place.' She stood up and walked toward the window. 'It's not raining frogs, the skies look clear. If it was an emergency, then Cari would come. Except – she can't, can she?' Lola turned to frown at my ankles. 'Ah-ha. It's almost time for the Games.' She nodded knowingly. 'Where's Archie?'

'That's the problem. He's gone. They've all gone.'

Lola squinted at me, her head tilted like a curious bird. 'All of them?'

I nodded.

'Right, then. Where are we going, and what are we doing? Cari is trying to work out how to recover them, I'm guessing, and you've been sent to fetch the most powerful magic user in Witchgorn.'

How did she guess? I folded a little. Although, her co-operation might make everything easier. I liked Lola – she had a rebellious edge.

'We've never failed before. That's what happened, wasn't it? Did you see who was on the other side? Was it Raventor? Or Seastone Keep? They always want to discredit us.' She had gathered a selection of oddments as she spoke; a cat toy went in to her bag, followed by a small red flower and a seashell. The book she was reading was tried, but then abandoned.

'I didn't see anyone. It was a cold, swirling portal, and it hurt – it frosted my arm if that helps?' I held out my arm to show her the beautiful, itchy scarring. 'The familiars were happy to enter, though.'

'Cheese. I bet they were melting cheese just out of sight. It works every time. Lead on. That's a pretty scar, luckily, as no one can heal it for you yet.' She gestured to the front door. I walked ahead to let myself out and was about to ask what she meant by it working "every time" when I caught her whisper.

'Dandelion.'

The cat returned to her feet. As Lola passed the crop of unseasonal vegetables, she paused. I tried to give her privacy, but couldn't help noticing that every leaf on them froze. That was certainly one way to preserve her crop. She'd lose some of the flowers, but a preservation spell should keep the edibles good for a few days. I desperately hoped we'd found a solution by then.

Chapter Six

Phoenix Feather was packed out. No one wanted to wait until tonight, it seemed. I'd thought that we'd have a chance to talk before the villagers overheard everything. Maybe the others had, but as Milla and I had failed in our duty, with no little aid from an attractive young man, we were being excluded. It would only be fair.

Lola sat on a chair, whose tattered fringing untwisted with every breath of the draft that always wound around my feet in there. I much preferred Pigs Might Fly, but not being able to see it from outside did make it a little tricky to use.

Plus, the cow-eyed boy might be a spy. He wouldn't be watching the village inn, full of villagers; he'd be watching Pigs Might Fly. But then, since our familiars had gone, I hadn't seen him at all.

'Shall I get you a coffee?' I asked Lola.

'Not from here. I'll have something stronger. I suspect I'll need it. I can't use any magic today anyway. Dandelion is worn out.'

Preservation was a tiny spell. Dandelion's age had been the

main reason Lola stepped down, but I hadn't realised his reserves were that low. All plans for asking Lola to create the illusion of a goat's male anatomy on Dusty faded into sleepy purrs. We were going to have to sew what was needed. Aran was right – we needed sleight of hand from the entire village if we were going to pull these Games off.

Lola didn't ask for any more details. She just sat calmly and waited. Eventually, the others started to arrive.

It was odd seeing the procession of animals on harnesses; far from the usual situation of each familiar freely roaming around their associate. Milla and her rabbit took a seat at the front of the stage. I considered joining them, but given my role and Lola's presence, I decided that I'd stay amongst the crowd. One by one, the others took their seats, coaxing, tugging, and bribing their associated animals to join them. All aside from Cari, who was still notably without a magpie.

Dusty pawed at the ground, unsettled by the crowd, and lowered her head at a passing villager. Dotty-The-Second decided that the stage was the perfect place to poo as Amy blanched in horror. It was an utter mess. Not one person in the village could be remotely convinced that these were our familiars.

Aran waved at me as he entered, and Royce followed. They sat right in front of the rest of my protectorate and waited.

Lola leant over to me. 'You really are in trouble. This will never work.' She sat back with a thoughtful expression and stroked Dandelion.

'Good afternoon, and thank you for coming.' Satu stepped forward with Dusty positioned behind her. I held my breath, expecting a head butt at any minute. 'I'm sure many of you noticed that we have a slight issue on our hands.'

'Your goat changed sex!' called a teenager from the side of the room.

Satu ignored them. 'Every year before the Games, someone will attempt sabotage. We have won them a few times recently, so we were targeted. They have acted earlier than expected, and we failed the test. At this point, we cannot know if it was just us, or if other villages were also affected. In fact, we cannot know for sure that the incident is even linked to the Games.'

'You don't know much at all!' came a shout from another area of the room.

Satu remained her usual calm self. Cari wasn't taking the centre stage yet, so they weren't worried. 'No, we don't.' She smiled. 'But we do know that if it is outside interference, you – as a village – are vulnerable.'

'To better witches who don't lose their familiars?'

'To all sorts. Do you want to be embraced as a territory of Seastone Keep? We're the only village this side of the chasm. If it's Raventor, they could be up to anything. Whatever the reason, somehow, we need to look as though everything is normal to any observer.'

A hum of conversation filled the room as people discussed the implications. Raventor's magic users were notoriously difficult the last time we held the Games. They expected to be treated as exceptions, to be almost worshipped by non-magic users. Satu had done well by mentioning them. And we already had to pay a small amount of peace money to Seastone Keep. All the villages did. It kept normal citizens from outside the Twin Chasms away from the rest of us. No one wanted to become a tourist destination for curious folk. We traded our food via Seastone Town and were left in peace. Paying a bigger tithe was almost impossible for most folk in Witchgorn.

Aran leant forward to speak to Satu, and she nodded.

Royce and Aran took the stage.

'Good lads, those,' Lola whispered. 'Good heads on them. They'll help calm things as long as the landlord here is onside.

She's the bigger influence in the village. Can get all sorts to listen to you when they're drunk and in debt.'

'Look, folk, this is right funny. I'd know – I've spent an hour watching Satu trying to catch Dusty here.' Royce gestured at the goat. 'But they're right. I don't want higher prices to pay or some nosey bastard from Seastone lording it over us. We get left alone out here, and that's how I like it.'

Murmuring assent from a few individuals.

'We need to fake it till they go away. We need to help the protectorate until they can fix the mess, and we get our normal life back. Heck, if Dusty can fake being a male goat for a few weeks, I can pretend that's what I see.'

I wasn't sure that Dusty had any choice in the matter, but I appreciated the way he was trying to go about it. He swept his gaze across the crowd, and as his eyes met mine, he paused, smiling before continuing.

'If you see anyone who isn't from here, you let myself, Aran, or Beth know. We'll deal with it.' Beth had come out from behind the bar and walked to the stage. She was a slender, petite woman with a will of iron. No one crossed her.

'You will pretend that these are the real familiars and address them as such,' Beth said, her hands resting on her hips, daring anyone to argue with her. There was a general nodding like bluebells in a spring breeze.

Aran took centre stage and did his sleight-of-hand trick. People laughed.

The teenager hollered, 'We've all seen you do that a hundred times. What are you trying to prove?'

'How many more of you can do it?' Aran asked. Two others put their hands up. 'Show me.'

One managed successfully, and the other fumbled it. Suddenly, I could see that it was all about hand movement, about clever positioning.

'This is what we need to do,' he said quietly. 'The village protectorate is so used to their magic that they could not see the reality of the trick, only the illusion of magic. Those coming to the Games will be the same. We need to work as a village to pull off the biggest show of illusion and tricks that has ever been done.'

Now the noise swelled, and those on the stage let it.

'I know how they could do one,' Lola said quietly. 'I think I'll get this started.'

She stood, and every voice quietened. 'Thank you. My voice is not so strong these days, but my memory is as good as any. As host of the Games, it is our responsibility to choose the events, and we have to notify all other villages by the end of this week what those will be. That gives us two days to decide what we believe we can pull off.' She paused for dramatic effect and gestured in the direction of the main village entrance.

'Out there is one of our biggest secrets. Our golem. The village founders didn't have the money that Seastone has or the natural resources of Westwick but they still wanted an imposing guardian. Our golem is one of the biggest – because it's hollow. Our predecessors could not afford the stone to make it solid. Therefore, I propose we choose the golem race as one of our games and work out how to move it from the inside.'

'Won't it rather dislike that?' Beth asked.

'I suppose we might tickle it in the process, but it won't be able to stop us. We'll just have to make it up to the golem later.' Lola shrugged.

I wasn't even sure golems could hold a residual consciousness for long enough to be upset. But the village tended to think in terms of moving things being sentient, and it was easier to let them.

Royce nodded. 'If it's hollow, we could rig up pulleys and

ropes. It would mean a few of us have to ride inside to make it work. We'll take volunteers for each event afterwards.'

Cari stepped to the front of the stage. 'Before tomorrow, we need serious ideas for how we could pull off the events. We hope that Lola can help us with a small spell each day, but aside from that, it needs to be entirely illusion based, or possible.'

Beth nodded and waved at the bar. 'Free drinks for everyone. Line 'em up boys – I think we'll need the inspiration.'

Chapter Seven

Several hours later, we'd decided on just two more events. Fencepost racing, where we flew a fencepost from one end of the field to the other, and bloom and grow, where the challenge was to grow the most fruit the fastest.

We had no idea how the village believed they were able to do them, but they assured us that both were within their capabilities – with a little help from Lola.

We still needed at least two more events. Fastest familiars had always been my favourite, but looking at those we had procured, I wasn't convinced we could attempt it. Well, not without a lot of cheese. It wouldn't be totally impossible, unless the duck or magpie didn't like cheese.

'I think we should do fastest familiars,' I said. Silence fell, and then the ripple of laughter started to grow, rolling around the room and gathering volume and momentum as it bore down on me.

Even Lola chuckled. 'Unless you have an incredible animal trainer, I really can't see how you have any chance of doing that.'

'We don't have to win, we just have to compete,' I replied. I'm sure we can do it with enough food bribes and lots of hard work. Dotty loves cheese – maybe enough to run after it. Doug is a trained herding dog. We only have to get one animal to run.'

'What about fire-flight?' one of the older farmers asked. She stared out the door with a wistful expression. 'We could make real fire and shoot it upwards, then it would look like you just cast the flames. Always thought there had to be a way to do that.'

Now I knew why I'd already had one fire call out, and Cari had appeared so exasperated by the woman every time she came into Pigs Might Fly.

'Or beanstalk growing! I can sew you the tallest beanstalk ever, and it can be pulled upward – slowly.' The young man who spoke was dressed in a veritable rainbow of colours, with frills and ruffs on every inch of his clothes. Larent could sew, but would something so huge fool magikers? The point we pulled any leading rope or thread over would have to be so high that I couldn't even begin to think where we could support it. While each of these could be possible, we needed to ration Lola's magic very carefully to pull it off.

'It needs to be perfect.' Cari looked at the young man intently.

'I can do it. Really, I can. I've always wanted to see just how far I could push my designs. I may only need a little help from Lola. Just to make the leaves rustle naturally.'

Cari nodded. 'Then we have our events. Fencepost racing, golem racing, fastest familiar, beanstalk growing, and fire flight. We could keep bloom and grow as a backup, but it's a bit too similar to beanstalk. Are you absolutely certain you can sew one?'

Larent gasped. 'Yes, thank you – I won't let you down!'

A small smile grew on the face of the fire-obsessed farmer, and I suspected we might be in trouble.

'I'll arrange delivery of the lists,' Satu said. 'Then, Pigs Might Fly must be rested until the event. There are many things we can fake and cast illusions of, but there is no way to engineer a wandering coffee shop without giving ourselves away. '

Aran stood. He gestured to be allowed to talk and Satu retired to her seat.

'Okay. We can't all meet as one group again. It looks too suspicious. As a magiker-watcher, I'd be wondering what was going on if they suddenly started frequenting the inn more often.' He blushed as he said it, but he was entirely right. 'Animal related assistance goes to Royce – Larent, before you start the beanstalk, could you sew some, umm, *male parts* for Dusty? If any of you with pig experience think you can figure out how to help train Dotty not to mess in public, and especially if you've caught a magpie, Royce is your first stop. Mistress Cari has been trying to befriend one, but if we're being watched, she can't be trudging round the woods bribing birds, so if you happen to get one, that would be great.'

Royce nodded. 'Don't rush me all at once, but pop over to the farm tomorrow.'

Aran pointed at Lola. 'If you want to be part of the golem team – if you think you can rig levers and pulleys, or work them faster than the magic-filled golem can run – see Lola. She knows how it works.'

Lola smiled and leant to whisper in my ear. 'This is going to be so much fun!'

'Sewing skills, see Larent. For everything else, come to any of us with your ideas. I suspect that our village protectorate have thoughts of their own, which they need to stew over. Oh, and I need spiders ... a lot of spiders.'

The meeting broke up slowly as people drifted back to their homes. Satu gestured me over.

'Walk back with me.'

We strolled back toward Pigs Might Fly. It was sunken on its floor in the middle of the field when I looked through Aran's mask.

'What happens when it starts to lose too much of its fuel?' I'd never realised that a building could look sad until now. Somehow, the shutters drooped and the roof looked saggy. It couldn't fall apart that fast, surely?

'It will become a fixed building.' Satu stroked the brick-work, and Pigs Might Fly creaked a window in acknowl-edgement.

'I won't let that happen to you, don't worry,' she murmured. 'The first familiar back will start to feed you, whether they like it or not.'

She grimaced, although her voice remained very calm – musical and sing-song. 'If we need to sustain Pigs Might Fly with Dandelion's magic to keep its awareness alive, then we will. But hopefully, we have a few weeks' grace there, as long as no one uses the magic for anything significant. Pigs Might Fly, you need to hold onto as much as you can – no walking! We need one last favour, then I want you to rest. We need to send the list of challenges to all the other villages through your fire. I'll light it myself, the old-fashioned way, then you need to send the list out in seared magic.'

A window shutter rattled in acknowledgment.

'What does that mean?' I knelt alongside Satu and helped her to build up a fire.

'The message will appear on the wood in their own fires. If there is no wood, then in soot on the wall. It's one of the only accepted methods. The other way requires enchanted flying letters, and we can't get those there in time, not with how hungry they are for magic.'

She struck a match, and the fire struggled to light, then it whooshed high.

Satu frowned. 'Don't waste your magic!' A charred stick fell from the fire, and the flames shrank to the small, natural flame just starting to catch light.

Satu wrapped her hand in her sleeve and picked up the stick, quickly scratching names of the challenges in the sooty wall at the back of the fire. She paused for a moment. 'I'm sorry, but it's well known in Two Chasms that Ralph races fastest familiar. He's won it so often that entering any other racer would make no sense. I don't think it's a good plan after all. We might be able to do dancing familiar.' Before I could respond, she'd scratched it into the wall.

'This is much harder with real, hot flames,' she grimaced as they started to lick upward.

'Ready.'

The fire blazed once more, covering the full height of her scratched writing. Despite the intensity of the flames, they gave out little heat as they changed through a series of colours.

'Each colour represents a different village,' Satu muttered, cradling her hand. I rose and collected a glass of water for her to cool her fingers in.

She took it gratefully.

'Thank you, Pigs Might Fly,' she said, then turned to me with narrowed eyes. 'Did you see how I did it? We all have a role in the protectorate, Eva. Once we get the familiars back, yours will be in here, with me, to help return life to our beloved cafe.'

I nodded. 'It would be my honour to serve you both.'

'It should not be so. You should be punished – stripped of responsibility. But instead, as you are not solely responsible, you will serve our servant. You will feed the cafe and the golem. You will repay the damage you will cause them by your lack of attention.'

I wondered what punishment Milla would get for leaving me alone. Sacrificing my own learning and magic to help the village keep both of our constructs felt a worthwhile use of my talents. Satu would probably fix all the other things that unravelled which I did not yet have the skills for.

<h1 style="text-align:center">Chapter Eight</h1>

The sun was just peeking out over the forest, spying on our preparations, as I reached Royce's farm the next day to spend some time with Doug the dog. Satu was already there with Dusty, who now sported a sizeable set of male genitalia.

In fact, I had to look twice to be sure that she was actually Dusty. On closer inspection, tiny stitches were visible, and the small metal rings bonding the furry top section of the genitals were tightly clasped around some of Dusty's actual hair.

Still, it wouldn't stand up to close inspection. Dusty raised a warning hoof, and recalling the last face full of mud this goat had given me, I stood up quickly.

As I peered from a distance, admiring the way they had hidden the udder, Satu coughed.

'When you've quite finished ...' she arched an eyebrow. 'You were lucky not to get a hoof in the face there. She caused Mathilda quite a problem when we attached them. It took Royce and two others to hold her still.'

'How are the others doing?' I glanced across the paddock in case Amy had brought Dotty-The-Second up for some help.

Milla and Fennel would be fine, and I suspected that Gail was still somewhere bribing Sirathon-The-Second to be her friend.

'We still have a magpie problem.' Royce grimaced. 'There's a whole flock of the blighters back in the woods, always stealing eggs and causing chaos. But I've spent my life chasing them away. Now, somehow, we have to get them to trust someone.'

Not just *someone*. Cari.

Crunching gravel gave away another visitor. Mathilda waved sheepishly at me. 'You were lucky she's never been in kid,' Mathilda said. Her usually perfect hair appeared rather more dishevelled than usual.

'You were too,' Satu replied.

'You did amazingly!' I gestured at Dusty's new genitals and tried really hard not to look at the black eye Mathilda was wearing. Usually, the village protectorate would have healed that easily, but all Dandelion's power was being reserved for other tasks.

'Thank you. I think it will do until the event, certainly from any distance we might be watched from, but it still needs tweaking for the day itself.'

I couldn't help but agree. Sirathon, and preferably Ralph, too, needed to find a way home as soon as possible. With enough bribes, we might have a small chance of faking the other familiars, but the birds were a whole different matter.

'You should pop by Milla's to help cover—' I started, but Satu elbowed me.

'—the trays of cookies I could smell. Maybe if you tell her you fixed Dusty, you can grab a couple?'

Mathilda offered a shy smile. 'Thank you, I'll do that,' she said, then walked in Milla's direction.

'Why not tell her?' I whispered.

'It's not a new bruise.' Didn't you notice the colour? For

some reason, she's had that a few days and not asked for healing. There's no way she doesn't know.'

I didn't recall seeing it at the meeting, but maybe she'd covered it, just as I'd been about to suggest. I'd keep a quiet eye on her.

Doug trotted out to Royce as he blew a small, shrill whistle. I crouched down to run my hands through his soft grey fur and scratch the warm spot behind his ear. Doug looked up at me and tilted his head expectantly.

'Of course.' I fished in my pocket for a treat, the scent of the meaty lump hitting my nose as soon as it was exposed to the air. Doug dribbled.

He took it gently, his teeth making the barest of contact with my skin, and then nudged at my pocket for more.

'For today, and for a few more days, use his lead, Mistress Eva.' Royce crouched to clip the tattered rope onto Doug's collar and handed it to me. It was rough and frayed at the end. A slight damp permeated the fibres, and I was sure it would smell if I put it too close to my nose.

'Thank you. We won't be long,' I said.

'You'll be as long as your treats last.' Royce laughed.

I had a lead. We'd be fine.

We weren't. I'd just got to Larent's front door when I ran out of treats. He waved me in, and Doug sat on the road, refusing to move.

'Doug, walk.' I tugged on his lead gently. He turned his head toward home.

Larent held up a bundle of green fabric to the window. More shades of green than I'd ever seen in one place. I crouched next to Doug, gently scratching at his ear and trying to coax him a little further.

He wasn't too big. I could carry Archie easily, so maybe I could carry Doug. A few minutes wouldn't hurt.

I tried to pick him up, but his paws paddled in the air, his legs kicked at my side, and he writhed in more slippery waves than any snake I'd ever seen.

Doug did not want to be picked up. He didn't bare his teeth or expose the whites of his eyes; he just wagged frantically and wriggled free.

I just about kept enough hold of him to ensure he didn't get hurt on landing, but in the process, lost the end of the straggly rope.

'Do you have any sausages?' I called frantically.

Larent laughed from the doorway. 'I don't. I'll see you later, Mistress Eva!'

I trudged after the furry, grey streak vanishing into the distance. I needed to carry far more treats. My pockets would be so full of sausage that every dog in town would follow me. Doug was a stomach on legs, and he'd be rolling home instead of running by the time we held the Games.

On my way back across the field, I passed a group of teenagers laughing as they ran toward the old barn. It had long been abandoned to mice and feral pigeons until today. Now it housed the golem team. Between the group, they dragged ropes and hauled pulleys with the lightness of youth. To them, it was a great game. The village protectorate had always been there. The implications of another village taking over were not entirely clear to them, but they joined in for the sheer fun. Better them than me. Although, I did really want to see how the final golem propulsion system – GPS for short – would work.

A stooped shadow and a cat stood in the doorway, urging them on. It was good to see the golem team were excited for their job – if only we could get the familiars so keen on their new roles. I walked after Doug with soaking shoes and the hem of my skirt dragging through wet grass.

Doug had reached Royce's house. Embarrassment preceded me up the path as I trudged my shame into Royce's paddock. He glanced up as I walked round the corner of his house.

'How far did you get? You were out longer than I expected.' Doug licked me, all innocence and wagging tail.

I missed Archie.

'He'll warm to you eventually. Stay for food if you want?'

'Thank you, but I should get back. I have a giant green plant to look at.'

Royce grimaced. 'Aran has shared his plans for most of the tricks, but that one ... I can't see how it will work yet. Too much fabric to hide in a heap on the floor, and I can't see how it will look real enough.'

I worried about it too. If I was honest, I was most worried about the fire dancing. I'd seen something glowing in the air about the height of the farm building at one point yesterday, and there had been a number of small fires today already, judging by the scent of smoke. True magical fires didn't smell, nor did they catch neighbouring barns alight.

Chapter Nine

To make it look as though the golem moved by magic, Amy stood in the big field with Dotty-The-Second by her side, freshly bedecked with ribbons and painted spots. The golem race would be across Pigs Might Fly's field, around the perimeter to the north, then back again. Our golem had never won. It was the tallest, but its lumbering stride was nothing to match the shorter, almost humanoid ones that Seastone Keep brought as guards. Those things could run.

We didn't need to win. We simply needed to compete. The trouble was that the golem crew would not just have to race, they would have to work it for the entire duration of the visit – and change the crews for rest and sleep – without being seen.

Lola beckoned me over excitedly when she spotted me staring. 'He doesn't like being moved, but he's tolerating it.' She gestured at a hole in the floor. A wooden trap door slid back when she tapped on it, and an eager teenager looked up at me.

'Is it our go? Oh, hi, Mistress Eva. I know I should be mad at you or something, but this is the most fun we've had in an age. We're about to change the crews over. Would you like a go?'

Lola coughed for attention, and the girl had the grace to look embarrassed.

'Sorry, Mistress Lola. I assumed ... well, you know, that you were a bit old to want a try.'

Lola laughed. 'Old is as old behaves, and working with all you young'uns makes me feel quite spritely. Maybe just a short journey, though?'

The girl's grin could have lit the barn as she called back into the tunnel.

'Two protectorate members up in the next run. Let's have some strength aboard, and shuffle back to let them in.' The heavy footfall of the golem approached the barn as Lola and I clambered down into the tunnel.

'This is very exciting,' she whispered. 'I was just growing plants, now I'm back designing things. Retirement is overrated.'

The trapdoor slid closed, and we were shuffled to one side of the freshly dug tunnel. A knock sounded on the wood, and the girl who'd invited us in slid it back, exposing a pair of feet. One after another, a whole group of the GPS dropped into the hole from inside the golem's leg.

'You'll need to climb up, one on each side of the torso, please. You can see pegs in the leg to climb, but don't get tangled in the ropes. Once you get far enough up, the torso team has small seats. They're folded up so we can all rotate within the shift time.'

'So we don't need to pull anything?' I'd really hoped to help move the golem, but I supposed seeing it work from the inside would still be special. A wiry boy pushed past me.

'I'll be shoulder left,' he called and started climbing the pegs inside the golem's legs, followed by a girl racing up after him.

'I'll have shoulder right.'

'You two are up next.'

Lola and I climbed up to the small seats inside the torso. In all the ridiculous skirts I had to wear, I found it hard to get enough of my backside on the small ledge. It was dark and claustrophobic.

'One perk of retirement is normal clothes.' Lola called over with glee in her voice.

Barely above my head, I could hear the feet of the person above me.

'Do you use light?' I whispered.

'When we're all in, we can light the neck-lamp. It makes his eyes glow like they usually do. We put a candle in it for now – there's a stock of them in your reach, Mistress Lola.'

From somewhere below me, a deep voice called. 'All in. Light up and let's run.'

The neck light spluttered into life, illuminating the pulleys and ropes that now articulated every part of the golem.

'Make sure they don't tangle,' the deep voice called. And we were off. As ropes were pulled, the golem slowly lurched forward as though it might topple at any moment. Frantic hauling on more ropes, pulleys spinning, and a head popped up as the front leg raised. They vanished a moment later as the leg dropped, and more frantic hauling of ropes and loosening of others ensued. Soon the panic settled, and after a few strides, I no longer felt certain that we'd topple over as the arm team worked to keep the golem balanced. I soon spotted which ropes were doing which task, and Lola and I lent our strength to the movement.

Onward we walked, step after lumbering step. It grew hot and sticky. Although they may have had the mechanics worked out – aside from removing pulleys without tickling a reawakened golem – there were a few things this bunch of keen kids had overlooked. If they were in here for hours, they needed water and the ability to relieve themselves in an emergency. The golem could hardly head to its shed every time one of the GPS needed a nature break. It needed to stand guard at the gate all day.

'Hold tight, we're going to run. Three steps and we pick up the pace! Three ... two ... one ...'

I grabbed the nearest climbing peg as the team started to pull ropes faster, their heads popping up and down as the legs lifted, the noise of grinding stone intensified as each joint was coaxed into movement. With one person on each main limb section, and eight in the golem in total, it was going to get hot, and fast.

'They need a mirror in here,' Lola muttered. 'If they had a mirror, they could see through the eyes from this seat. Someone could direct the team from inside.'

'Who's directing us now?' I called out.

'Thirty-five steps to the fence, left turn, twenty steps—'

'That's very impressive, but what if another golem, or any other creature, gets in your way?' We slowed until we came to a gentle rest as the right leg voice replied.

'That's a good point, actually. I mean, we started just trying to move this thing between us, and we did it. If we can see for ourselves, we could roam around more easily instead of trying to count or hear Amy over a crowd.'

By the time we returned to the shed, my skirts were stuck to my legs as though I'd been wading in the pond again. It made getting back out of the golem's foot hole tricky, and my skirt caught on a rough patch of stone as I squeezed out.

Lola led me back along the tunnel to another exit at the far side of the barn.

The cool breeze outside was a welcome relief from the sweaty stench of the golem. The GPS team had done it; I could not doubt that. We had a racing golem and one of the games was going to be okay. There were just a few small issues to work out, and one of those could be fixed with a few water bags. As I looked at the group of sweaty, tired teenagers leaving the barn, it occurred to me that a more subtle entrance and exit might be needed.

We probably didn't have either the time or resources to make a longer tunnel stable enough to use, but maybe a few of the farmers on the edge of the village could create a structure that looked like an actual house? Then a group of teens might have a reason to be meeting up, and visitors a reason not to be in there.

Chapter Ten

It was nice to have Lola in the meeting. With everyone's disapproval still clearly aimed at myself and Milla, Lola diffused the tension with her enthusiasm.

'Did you see how fast they can run?' She chortled as she held her sides. 'It was amazing!'

Amy sat with Dotty-The-Second; she had a strong fragrance of cheese about her person and attracted sideways glances from Dusty as much as the pig. Dusty was, as expected, every bit as cantankerous as Jerry and resisted all attempts to make her answer to that name. Given the little time we had left, she was not helping matters.

The entire room smelled of bribes. My own pockets bulged with sausages, and the various seeds on Gail's clothing led to the duck pecking her frantically.

'This is ridiculous,' Cari muttered. 'Look at us. We can't fool anyone like this.'

'We just have to hold out until Ralph gets back. Then we can find our familiars and bring them home,' Satu muttered as she tried to stop Dusty from wandering down the stairs.

'I take it one of you rushed up and read the portal straight after the kidnapping?' Lola asked.

Cari shook her head. 'We were too shocked, caught out.'

'There might be some residue left – if you'd let me have a look?'

'We can't waste what magic you can use.' Cari smiled at Lola. 'We won't let you draw too much from poor Dandelion. I'm sure he was enjoying retirement.'

Lola looked at me and raised an eyebrow before turning back to Cari. 'When I was in charge—'

'But you aren't. We need you and we need to look after you.'

Lola crossed her arms, and Dandelion swished his tail back and forth. 'Well, I may as well go and ride in a golem then. At least I can be helpful there. Used for more than Dandelion's magic. Plus, it's fun.'

'Lola, we do need you and Dandelion here.' Satu reached over to lay a soft hand on Lola's arm, easing her back to her chair. 'We need a charm for growth and bounty.'

It was enough to distract Lola from her intention to flounce away.

'Growth and bounty, you say? I'm intrigued.' She sat back down.

'Aran has been collecting spiders. He's had all the village children gathering them. Half of his sleight of hand tricks appear to involve an almost invisible thread, and I suspect I know what he plans to do with those spiders. If you could talk him out of making them *too* big ...' Satu grinned. 'Although, a plague of giant spiders might stop visitors from delving too deep into our secrets.'

'Talking of secrets.' I needed to ask while we had time to build. 'I think we need to offer one or two of the older golem team members a new house. We can't have them coming out of the shed looking as though they've just done exercise in a very small space for a long time while others go in.

Milla laughed. 'We could fill the room with heavy things, like sacks and rope swings, cans of paint and fenceposts. All that stuff they throw around in the field to try to improve their muscles.'

It was a good idea. 'It would certainly give them a reason to go in there, and a reason to look a mess when they come out.' Milla was definitely growing on me.

She plunged on with her idea. 'We could put a sign up! Call it *Grow Your Muscles*. I think you're right. It needs people living there to keep it private so no out-of-town visitors come wandering in.'

'Paulie and Tom are courting – we could make it theirs.' I'd seen them holding hands as they walked to the golem shed.

Milla snorted. '*Courting*? Eva, I forget how old you are sometimes! We don't say courting these days.'

She hadn't rejected it out of hand, nor had any of the others.

'We need a fast house built for containing our teenagers' muscle-building antics?' Satu nodded. 'It's a good idea.'

'That means they need to be actively using the barrels in the fields for a week or so where they can be seen. Anyone's familiar could be flying overhead.' Amy stroked Dotty-The-Second thoughtfully. 'It would be easy enough to set that up.'

'I wish it was mine.' Cari sighed. 'Blooming magpies. We'd also need to extend the tunnel slightly to reach past the shed and into the private area of a new building. All in favour?'

Every member of the protectorate raised their hand aside from Gail, who raised a duck.

'All in favour of using Dandelion's magic today on the spiders?'

Lola was the only one who didn't agree here. 'I think you

should check the portal signature. The spiders can wait. If Dandelion can scent the pattern or function, you can get working on a plan. Then, as soon as that ridiculous magpie returns, you can get working on the portal.'

We were putting a lot of hope in Ralph's intelligence. I bribed Doug down the steps and back out into fresh air. As long as he had sufficient sausage, he would behave perfectly. I should really take him home, but as far as I could see, there was no way for him to stay at my house. His scratching at the door for freedom drove me mad. He was so fast and into everything. Archie was calm – my constant companion – and my soul felt empty without him.

I didn't care about the magic anymore. I just wanted my dog back.

Lola started walking away from Pigs Might Fly toward the top field near the duck pond. The one I'd lost the familiars in.

'Come along, girl. I want to know what you know and see what you saw. Spare me no details. I know they want spider thread, but this is too important. We need to know how to get them back, or you may as well pack up and move to Seastone Keep today. It wouldn't be long before they have you sat in one of their little chambers, enchanting potion after potion for them to sell in the far lands as a natural remedy. People without magic are far more willing to believe in fallacy and claims of a dubious nature when it comes to their health than they are magic.

'One time, I sold a bottle to a woman, claiming it contained a dream berry that would help her sleep. I simply cast a delayed sleep spell on her. She was delighted, and before long, everyone wanted dream berry drinks. Anyway, what I'm saying is that we want to get your dog back.'

'They must get breaks at Seastone?' I asked, as I scrambled over the fence. Lola frowned and walked to the gate.

'They get changes, rather than breaks – they just make something different,' she replied. 'Now where was this portal ... oh.'

The streak of frost-killed grass marked the portal clearly.

Lola crouched down, reaching for the shrivelled, dead vegetation. 'What did it look like?'

I described it to the best of my memory, including the frost creeping up my arm.

'But all the familiars made it through? None of them touched it?'

'That was the strangest thing. They flew through – even Dotty.'

She sat in the grass and called Dandelion over. He stalked up, rubbing his chin across her legs.

'I'm inclined to say this is too showy for Seastone Keep.' She reached for Dandelion and plonked him unceremoniously in her lap. 'I also think that whoever did this will want to see this scar here when they arrive as proof of success.'

'It's a job for the offcuts from Larent's beanstalk maybe?' I suggested. 'Lola, what will they do to our familiars?' Now we were away from the others, I hoped she'd be willing to share more than they did.

'Or paint. With a few strands mixed in.' She sat up and looked at me. 'If it's just a pre-Games test, then there are two options. The village watches us struggle, we are exposed as having failed, they then return the familiars at the end.'

'What's the point?'

'Humiliation, a warning that we were not alert enough,

unready for a true threat. The second is an attempt at a hostile takeover after exposing us.'

Like Raventor and Mistead. I held down panic, focused on breathing slowly. Archie was still alive. 'What would they do to our familiars?

Lola frowned. 'No one would ever hurt another magiker's familiar. It's well past the codes of engagement. We'd simply be exiled to Seastone Keep as a group unfit to be a working protectorate.'

'If it's not a pre-Games test?'

'Then we're all in danger. But, as no one has felt any of their familiars in pain, I'm confident it's not rogues. Give me a moment's quiet now, Eva. I need to get ready. Can't waste a drop of Dandelion in these circumstances.'

She sat so still and quiet with her hands buried in the grass that I thought she'd fallen asleep. I waited, more unsettled by her words, almost wishing I'd not asked.

Eventually, as the sun started to sink behind the hill, Lola opened her eyes. She sighed deeply.

'Take Dandelion back to my house, would you? Tell the knocker to let you in. I need to have a conversation with Cari.'

She didn't wait for a reply, but handed me a sleeping cat and walked away.

Chapter Eleven

With Dandelion returned, it was time to take Doug home.

Royce sat on his porch in a rickety chair, waving as we drew close. Doug strained at his lead. Any hope of the sausages keeping him by my side had long gone.

Dusty was starting to behave as well as any goat ever would; Dotty-The-Second was so obsessed with food that she had little thought in her brain for anything else. But Doug, he loved Royce.

As we drew closer, light glinted off Royce's glasses. Something about him looked a bit different.

'Let him go,' he called, and I released the lead. Royce whistled, and Doug shot through the grass, his tail wagging so hard I thought he might take off. He leapt into Royce's arms, leaving his clean shirt covered in paw prints.

Ah. That was it. Royce looked clean. His clothes had no mud on, and his glasses weren't smudged.

He laughed as he looked down at his now mud-smeared clothes.

'Well, I did try,' he said as I drew closer. 'How did today go? Have a seat.'

A second chair sat in the thin evening sun. I tested it surreptitiously, and it felt stable, so I sat.

'I went in the golem.' I couldn't hold the grin back. 'It was so much fun. We found a few small issues with changeover, but they're in hand. We just need a quick house built.'

'Would you like some food?' Royce glanced toward his door as he asked.

'I wouldn't want to impose. I'm sure I could get myself something once home.' It was very kind of him, but the scent of sausages around me all day had dulled my appetite.

'How about a slice of bread and some soup, then? I made more than enough for myself.'

'If you're sure.'

Royce didn't need more encouragement. He sprung to his feet and pushed the front door open, returning moments later with a small table. 'It's lovely out here,' he said as he unfolded it.

He vanished inside again. I tested the table; it wobbled a little. While Royce was inside, I tucked a large pebble under one of its feet. The aroma of fresh bread wafted out the door.

Royce returned a few minutes later carrying a plate laden with thick slices of bread dripping with butter. 'I'll be right back.'

He scurried away, whistling as he returned with two bowls of a grey-brown soup. A swirl of cream decorated the middle of each.

'I found a bunch of mushrooms in the wood today. They looked too good to pass by.' He sat and passed me a spoon. 'Tuck in.' Royce dunked a slice of bread in his bowl.

I reached for a slice, finding it soft and warm. The butter dripped into my soup.

It was altogether delicious. As the sun dropped, we ate

companionably. Doug sat at Royce's feet, occasionally diving forward to snuffle up a dropped crumb. It was the calmest I'd felt in days.

I wiped the last drops of soup from my bowl and sat back.

'That was tasty.'

Royce shrugged. 'Figured with all the work you'd been doing, you probably didn't have much time for good food.'

'Thank you – you were right. Can I help clear up?'

Royce shook his head. 'Two bowls and a plate doesn't need helping. I'll see you in the morning.' He stood a little awkwardly as I gathered my skirts up.

It was nice out here, I let myself relax. I crouched to stroke Doug before turning to walk away from the small farmhouse, back to the village. Tomorrow, I'd need to look in at the beanstalk properly.

Aran met me at the entrance to Larent's house the next morning. He frowned as I approached.

'Where's Doug?'

'I haven't got him yet.'

Aran scratched at his beard. He looked a little unkempt and tired, his facade of easy ignorance wiped clean, and the man underneath exposed for his real intelligence and determination. 'You can't be wandering around without a dog, Mistress Eva. You need him around, like you always have Archie.'

'I'll deal with it in a bit. Can I see the beanstalk?'

'Would you usually visit Larent? Don't answer. I already know – you wouldn't. You'd be out in the morning, walking with Archie, then you go to Pigs Might Fly. After, you might go to your mother's.'

He shook his head at me. 'Mistress Eva, you still don't get it, do you? I know you feel responsible, and the others have told you to fix this, but you can't behave differently. You're going to have to trust us. *All* of you need to trust us. If you want to help, walk Doug, and collect me some more spiders. Take them to Beth.'

He turned his back on me and knocked on Larent's door.

'We need grass and paint or dye,' I said. I wasn't going anywhere until I knew the portal scar was being dealt with.

'Lola already asked. Go walk Doug. I'll catch up with you in Pigs Might Fly later.'

Larent opened the door. 'Ahh, you're here for your shirt fitting?' he asked Aran very loudly. Aran nodded as Larent opened the door to let him in. He winked at me and closed it.

I huffed as I turned in time to see Milla walking my way. 'They won't let us in,' I moaned as she drew close. Her makeup was a little less wobbly this morning, and the rabbit was very wiggly. She struggled to keep it calm.

'Fennel not being quite so good today, then?' I was glad to see someone else was struggling. Amy had been out and about less than normal, but I'd heard a few choice words as I passed her house last night. I'd no idea what Satu had done to Dusty, but that goat was behaving unexpectedly well in public – especially given her udder must be rather cramped.

Milla grimaced. 'I tried another rabbit – bad choice. Now I'm stuck with it until I have a reason to go home.'

'You could take some cookies to the Phoenix Feather?'

She shook her head. 'They had a full plate yesterday. Did you see the fires last night at the farm?'

'No. How bad was it?'

She sighed. 'There's absolutely no way we're going to get away with it. There was smoke, and it smelled hot and burning. They had pretty colours, I'll give them that, but they were in no real pattern. The fireballs need to be in a circle at the least, not a sky splat.'

So, all we still had was a golem.

'Aran asked for spiders. I'm going to collect Doug and look for some. Do you want to come?'

Milla's eyes widened. 'I think I'll leave that to you. I'm going to paint grass while a rabbit eats. I thought I'd take a few familiars up to the top field to eat, like we did—'

'Amy will appreciate the break.' I patted her on the arm. 'It will be fine. Did you ever see that cow-eyed boy again?'

'No, but I'm hoping it might draw him out.' She blushed. 'I know it was probably linked. But he was pretty.'

'He had big eyes and probably charmed you,' I retorted.

Milla skipped as she ran up Amy's path. 'Probably. If he turns up at the Games, I'll charm him back.'

I swallowed my reply. She had to behave normally, as I did. It was time to gather Doug.

Last night's rain soaked the hem of my skirts as I dragged them through the long grass. Doug was barking, and Royce's whistle carried across the thin, cold air as I drew closer. They were bringing the goats back from the woods as I reached the paddock. Doug bounded over and licked my hand before nudging my leg.

'You don't want me, you want the sausage,' I said before offering him a chunk. He took it and ran straight back to Royce.

'Doug, you just ate!' Royce bent over and scritched at Doug's ears. 'Did you eat?' This time, directed at me.

'Yes. Aran sent me over and won't let me see anything else.'

I tried to hide my frustration as I leant against the fence. 'I need to take Doug for a walk and collect spiders.'

'I'd come with you, but I hear there's a house needs building.' Royce gestured over at the old barn. 'While we're at it, I think the plan is to get a few things ready for Aran's spider-silk ropes. Hide the pulleys in the trees, that sort of thing. If you head out to the wood's edge, there's a few big bushes not far from the goat sheds. Lots of flies means lots of spiders.'

I looked over at where he pointed. It looked possible to get there without wading through the paddock.

'You can get his lead from inside the door if you want. It's open. I just need to finish up here.'

'Thank you. I'll wait.' I wasn't going to just wander into his house. Nothing was that much of a rush. Royce nodded. 'Suit yourself.' He wiped his hand through his hair, leaving a muddy streak across his glasses again.

'We could fix your eyes, you know. When we have everyone back.'

He frowned. 'What's wrong with my eyes?' As I looked at him, he burst out laughing. 'I'm sorry. Satu offered years ago. I'm sure you could, but I don't want to rely on magic to see. These do me just fine.' He ushered the last goat into the shed and swung the gate shut behind them. 'It's due to rain, so you'd best get going. Come along, Doug.'

He reached inside the door and handed me the lead. 'One moment ...' Royce swung the door wide open to reveal a small, cosy house. Aware of my dripping wet skirt, I fixed Doug's lead to his collar while Royce vanished into the next room. He returned with a tin. 'For the spiders.' He closed the door and set off toward the old barn. Doug pulled after him briefly, but once bribed with a sausage, soon stopped tugging, and we headed for the woods.

Chapter Twelve

The Phoenix Feather was quiet when I arrived with my spiders. Beth took one look at the tin and gestured for me to follow her. The sturdy bar hid a trapdoor and a set of steps, and a cold draft caressed my face as I followed her into the dimly lit cellar. Aran stooped under the low ceiling.

Skittering noises came from a collection of jars and tins on the shelf, while a net of flies in the corner buzzed loudly enough to put my teeth on edge.

'Why in here?' The idea of so many flies under the inn made my skin crawl. What if things got out of hand?

'Because I come in here all the time, because all the village does.' Aran ducked under a beam. 'How did you do?'

I handed over the jar and he cracked it open to peer inside.

'Mistress Eva, these are real beauties! That one has wonderful stripes. Lola will be here for lunch soon, and I'm hoping she can make the threads slightly thicker and much stronger. Then we'll get them rigged up to the pulley system.' He put them on the shelf. 'Did you have a nice walk?'

'Yes.'

'What was wrong with Milla's rabbit today? It looked like it didn't want to be with her?'

Gods but his eyes missed nothing. If he was noticing things like that, then so would other observers; we weren't going to pass as not having lost the familiars. We had another week and a half to get through. Two weeks before the Games, but there was always a chance people arrived early. We couldn't risk that – we simply weren't ready.

'I think it was probably just gas,' I replied.

He nodded. 'Shall we go up and get some lunch? I want to tell you about the projects, and I know you're desperate to hear about them.'

Beth led the way back up, dropping the trapdoor down after us.

'Mistress Eva, promise me that when you get your familiars back, these spiders and flies will be dealt with. We're not due a visit from Licensing anytime soon, but if the villagers want to keep buying Nevsern's ales, they have to approve us.'

Satu stood at the bar with Dusty calmly alongside her 'I'll deal with it personally, Beth,' she said. 'Please, could I have a coffee and one of Ma Russet's cookies? I daren't ask Pigs Might Fly.' She leant close to me. 'As Cari still hasn't caught a magpie, I suggest you have a drink first too. She's not in a particularly tolerant mood today.'

We took a small table in the corner where we could see the door. Dusty glowered, and each time someone entered, she lowered her head and scraped at the floor.

Beth sat with us, and one of the bar staff brought us a selection of cookies and a big flask of coffee.

'Aran, we need updates. I can't go to the meeting without something,' I said.

He pulled himself up, growing in confidence as he spoke.

'The beanstalk is incredible. It's currently looks about half the height of the one we grew last time. We probably can't get much taller, or we can't pull it up. Once the team finishes working on the tunnel to the new building, they'll make a pit to coil the beanstalk in.'

'That needs to be in place by the end of the week.' Satu frowned. 'How do you plan to lift it up?'

Beth grinned. 'I've got that under control. There's a gas maker in the cellar. If we bury it in the pit, then we can mix the components, and ta-da! Bubbles.' She took a powder and a liquid from her pockets, then poured them into the now-empty milk jug. Bubbles foamed from it, overflowing onto the table.

It was utterly brilliant. Unlike the others in the group, I'd been so late blooming my magic that I suppose I'd taken for granted what could be achieved without it. Satu, on the other hand, had used her powers since she was a child. This was probably the first time in her memory she'd had to function without it. She reached out to touch the bubbles.

'They smell a little strong. How will that work?'

I unlaced my boots and pulled off a sock, quickly pouring some of the mix into a glass and shaking it before popping the sock over the top. The gas slowly inflated the sock until it stood on end.'

Satu laughed. 'Well, that's not something I expected to see today. With a less hole-filled material, I can see how that would work. What about the fencepost racing?'

Aran nodded his head toward the floor. 'That's what the spiders are for – pulleys and threads. It's going to be a big job, and we really need Lola's help for a day or two. We need the silk to be stronger.'

'I'll make sure she stops by later.' Satu took a deep breath. 'The fire dancing isn't going so well, though, is it?'

'That depends on your perspective.' Beth took a long sip of her coffee, a sparkle in her eye as she carried on. 'Leesa is having a great time trying to make it work. Her father is less happy after last night's fire. It's possible, I think. But if we only have a few days left before it gets risky or visitors start to arrive, then the devices might need smell or sound cloaking magic to make them less obvious. It needs a few more days. We need to slow the arrivals.'

I pulled my sock back on, ignoring the very slight dampness. The coffee was strong and sweet. Doug begged at my side for crumbs with paws on my leg as his nose snuffled the air, so I broke a small bit from my cookie and sneaked it to him. He licked my fingers afterward and started to nudge at the pocket full of sausage.

Satu raised her eyebrow at me. 'Well-behaved familiars do not beg.' She stood, and Dusty took that moment to show that she was also not a familiar.

Larent entered the bar, all flounce and flapping fabric. Dusty immediately turned to face him, and in direct defiance of Satu's frantic commands, lowered her head and charged. Larent left the room twice as fast as he arrived. The door barely closed behind him in time to meet Dusty's horns.

He peered in the window. Dusty turned her focus there instead. Satu rushed over and dropped a rope around her neck, twisting it up over her nose as Dusty's nostrils flared.

'I think now would be a good time to head to our meeting,' she called back to me.

I drank the last of my coffee, and Doug walked with me on a loose lead to the door. Once we'd reached the main road, Larent re-appeared around the side of the building and dashed inside.

Gail and Amy sat together as we entered, with Dotty-The-Second and the constantly-eating-duck nearby. Once we'd shared our news with the rest of the group, Gail and Amy whispered together.

'We've been thinking,' Gail said. 'Everyone else is constantly with their fake familiars.'

'Except you,' Amy finished.

Cari looked up from the notes she had been making. 'That's a good point, Eva. Why is Doug not living at your house? Everyone else is suffering the inconvenience of your mistake, the whole village is working to hide it, and you just wander around minus a familiar half the time.'

'It would be even more obvious if he was at my house crying all night for Royce,' I replied. 'He didn't like being away from Royce for a few hours, let alone all night.'

Lola smirked. 'The other village magikers don't know you. You were older when you realised what you had in Archie.'

'Or too stupid to see it,' Amy whispered to Gail.

'Enough.' Lola settled them down with a glance. 'What I'm saying is that she could have been wed before she bloomed. It's happened before.'

I didn't like where this was heading.

'You should move in with Royce until this is over. It's the obvious solution.'

'Does he get a say?' The farmhouse was small, and I really couldn't see that there was much room.

Cari shook her head. 'It's for the good of the village. He will say yes. You simply need to stay in the same house. I do not expect to see you without Doug again until Archie is back. On that note, Lola, please go fix the spiders. Amy, I need your help. I'm almost there with the list of components we need to recreate the portal. The moon glow mushrooms need to dry before we can use them, so the sooner you can locate and pick them, the better. That way, as soon as Ralph gets here, I can cast it.

'Gail, we need to find a way to slow down travel. Take a trip to the chasms and check the bridges can't be persuaded to topple into the canyon. It would add at least a day to visiting travel if they have to retrieve them or deplete their magical stores so that things are a little less apparent.

'And lastly, talking of obvious, Dotty's spots are starting to crack and flake. She needs a better dye. Milla, your skills with makeup might make things last longer than whatever paint Amy has used. Please see to it that Dotty's spots do not budge. There are also a number of women in the village who look more scruffy than usual. I'd like to see that fixed. If you can't do it with magic, please get practicing and do it the non-magical way.'

She stared around at us all. 'Why are you still here? Satu, I'd like a quick chat about the portal.'

As one, we rose to our feet to head out and do as we'd been instructed. Well, the others did.

I liked my bed, my cosy house. I dragged my feet a little as I trailed them down the stairs. Royce was nice, but it was just a really big thing to ask of anyone.

'Can I move into your house and borrow your dog?' I shook myself, it wouldn't be fair to let everyone down. The whole village had pulled together to hide our vulnerability, so I had to go and see a man about a dog.

<h1 style="text-align:center">Chapter Thirteen</h1>

'You could try taking him to your house first?' Royce suggested. 'He's never been away from me at night, but he likes you. He might be fine.'

Royce was knee deep in straw, cleaning out the shed when I'd found him. Doug was stomach-deep, trying to snuffle up some form of dung.

'Leave.' Royce's tone was calm and measured. Doug immediately responded, sitting back on his haunches and looking at Royce for the next command. He was very well trained for a non-familiar, but only for Royce.

I drew a deep breath. The others were right. It wouldn't have to be for long – a week or two at most – and Royce wasn't unpleasant company.

'I think, if you can accommodate me, I'll be just fine on your sofa.'

He frowned. 'No, that won't do. You have my bed, and I'll sleep on the sofa. Once I've sorted all my jobs out, been to visit the new house, and checked in with Satu and Dusty, I'll pop back and sort the room out. Bring your stuff over before supper.'

This was going to be awkward, but I resolved to make the best of it. Royce pointed at a pitchfork that leant against the wall near me.

'If you give me a hand, I can get going sooner.'

I grabbed the old tool, its wood worn smooth from years of use, the prongs clean and well maintained. Not a spot of rust decorated anything in here. Together, we banked up the sides of the goat shed with a thick layer of straw. Doug lay behind us, facing out and keeping the goats from disturbing our efforts when a few drew close.

Royce passed me his fork and heaved the rest of the bale back into a barrow. 'Put those in the tool shed,' he said, pointing at the small storeroom before wheeling the remains over to the rest of his stores.

If I was supposed to live here, I needed to get familiar with the whole place. Trailing straw from my skirt, I carried the tools into the neat, pristine tool shed. Every item had its place. No dust or straw dared encroach past the entrance, feed buckets were clean and blades oiled. I stopped as I took it in. Royce's house looked tidy when I'd seen through the door yesterday, his life almost a direct contrast to the image he presented to the world. Royce clearly cared a lot more about his farm and home than he did about himself – or other people's perception of him.

Two empty spots on the wall exposed the homes of the forks. I carefully put them back, picking at the stems of straw caught around mine before I retreated outdoors.

Royce had called the goats, and they charged over. In Dusty's absence, another goat had risen to the pinnacle of the goat grumpiness mountain. This rust-coloured beast changed course as it drew close, veering toward me. Head down and snorting, it closed the gap rapidly.

'Hey-up there, Cuddles, no need for that. Mistress Eva will be living with us for a while, so you can stop your tantrum.'

Cuddles paused. Not for long, but long enough that Royce got hold of him and changed his course back to the goat shed.

'Cuddles?' I asked.

'I hand reared that one. He used to be very sweet when he was small. In fact, he was sweet until he felt he needed to be in charge.' Royce sighed. 'Dusty might be a pain, but she's my pain of a goat. We had an understanding, and I'll be glad to have her back.' I suspected Satu would be glad to hand her back too.

'I should go and pack, I suppose.'

Royce picked straw from his hair. 'Would you like to see inside the house first?'

I'd have time enough for that later. 'No, but I'd quite like to see the new house that's being built for the grow-your-muscle club on my way back home.'

'Then we'd better get underway if you want to see it in daylight.'

We left the paddock and, with Doug scampering alongside us, walked across the field to the old shed.

It was amazing how much could be achieved – and just how fast – when the village worked as one. All the walls were up, and the separate rooms identifiable. Paulie and Tom stood at the threshold to the unroofed building, holding hands and grinning like fools.

'This is amazing! We can't believe we get to keep this.' Paulie gestured at the wooden walls rising fast amidst the team of villagers.

'I never imagined we'd get our own place, let alone all these people working to build us one in a week. It's perfect – it has all the muscle-building stuff and a secret passage!' Tom shook his head. 'I'm so grateful, I can hardly put it into words.'

Everywhere we looked, villagers were cutting wood and painting walls, even before the roof was completed. The main beams for that were up, and I strongly suspected the main shed was now missing a large amount of its internal partitions.

From the corner of my eye, I saw motion near the fence. Were we being spied on?

I pointed at it without saying anything and put Doug on his lead. As we drew closer to the motion, a curly tail stuck up in the air. Amy and Dotty-The-Second were crawling around in the long grass across the field. She was counting.

'Sixty-four ... Sixty-five ...'

'What are you doing?' I didn't get too close in case I scared something away.

She huffed in frustration. 'Moon-glow mushrooms, but this pig is eating more than I can gather. Dotty picks things and puts them in the basket, gently and with care. This ... *thing* tramples them, rendering them useless.'

As she spoke, the pig nudged her over into a heap and took a mouthful of the mushrooms from Amy's basket. Amy squealed, Dotty-The-Second squealed, and the skies opened. Rain poured down. The practicalities of our huge skirts with their many pockets for not mixing spell components did not extend to rain, and very soon, we were drenched.

Dotty's spots had started to wash off, and Doug had rolled in a particularly muddy patch. As nice as Doug was, Archie would never have done that.

I hoped Archie was okay, that they were feeding him carefully.

Up in the sky, a dark shape flapped past, stark against the

clouds, but the rain was too heavy to be sure what it was. It was easy enough to dismiss the shape being a magpie. One of those birds really needed to escape soon.

Even when the portal was made, we'd have to entice them through it. As we sat in pouring rain, trying to collect tiny blue mushrooms, the differences between our familiars and these substitutes were stark. With Archie and Dotty, we'd have had four sets of eyes and the job completed in no time. Instead, we scrabbled around in the dirt, our attention split between collecting our own resources and trying to salvage another patch of the precious ingredients from the pig.

By the time the rain stopped and the scudding clouds revealed the moon, we had collected eighty-eight mushrooms. In the moon's light, we discarded several that didn't glow.

'Thank you. Have a great night in your new home,' Amy said, her thanks laced with an edge of spikiness. 'I wonder how many days it will take you to look as filthy as Royce.' She hoisted the basket over her arm and tugged the pig after her as she walked off to Pigs Might Fly's general area, leaving Doug and me to go pack.

The second I closed my front door, Doug shook. Mud and water sprayed all over my hall. I took him off the lead and wandered into my bedroom to gather as many clothes and essentials as I could fit into one bag. I'd need at least a week's worth of stuff. As I packed, Doug's whimpering grew from a gentle scratching at the door, through a rising whine, until it reached a full howl.

We'd made the right call. There was no way he could stay the night here – no one in the houses to either side would have a chance of sleep. I tried to settle him down, but it was to no avail.

Instead, I shoved everything I could see into the big bag and slung it over my shoulder. It would be easy enough to pop back for anything I'd missed.

With Doug back on his lead and straining at its full extent, we traipsed across the dark field.

We were halfway to Royce's when a whizzing sound rose into the sky to my left, and a bloom of fire illuminated everything. A circle of white lights exploded outward with a bang, and a moment later, another ring – this time green – inside it. It was beautiful, but too loud, and smoke hung around the lights. I had to admit it was better than anything I'd expected the village to come up with. Maybe, with a little bit of help from Lola, we could hide the scent or sound.

Doug had stopped. He quaked at my feet. I adjusted the bag and crouched down to fuss over him. His small nose nudged against my hand, and a rough tongue curled around my finger.

'It's all okay, boy. Doug, come.' He lifted his eyes back to mine at the command and walked alongside me, sticking much closer than before the fire-art had graced the sky.

Chapter Fourteen

We were greeted by a flustered Royce.

'You shouldn't knock, Mistress Eva,' he muttered. 'You're supposed to live here.' He glanced down and started to fuss over the dog. 'Is Doug okay? He's panting.'

'I was being polite. At this time of night, you think they've decided to spy on us? If they're already watching the village, and they notice this is my first night here, then knocking is the least of our worries. Our cover is already well and truly blown. Doug was upset by the fire flight.'

Royce shook his head. 'I knew they planned another try tonight. They'd been scouring the books on stacking the fire pellets inside a capsule yesterday. Did they manage an actual shape?'

I took a seat, dropping my bag by a chair. 'They made two circles, one inside the other. But it smells, and it makes a noise.' I gestured at Doug. 'It was clearly not magic. It's never going to work.'

Royce shrugged. 'We may not need it, but best to be ready.'

He pulled the table across before sitting. Doug immediately jumped onto his lap. 'I saw you hunting for mushrooms long after I left. Didn't think you'd want to eat them after that. Would goat's cheese and broccoli soup do instead? I had some in the cold-house that I made a day or two ago.' He grinned a little sheepishly. 'I like making soup, but it's not all I eat, I promise.'

'Thank you, that would be lovely.' I'd forgotten about the cold-houses and cupboards. It wasn't my job, so it was easy to forget how much else in this village relied on magic. They'd all be getting warm soon.

How long did Pigs Might Fly have left? I shuddered.

Royce returned with a steaming bowl of soup. It smelled amazing. He wandered off into another room, leaving me in peace. Doug trotted at his heels with his tail wagging happily.

Today's food was every bit as delicious as the mushroom soup. The sharp tang of goat cheese mingled with the broccoli beautifully. I'd need to steal his recipes before I moved back home.

My new house was minimal, but tidy. There were some tins on the shelf and a lovely ornament that looked magic-wrought in pride of place over the fire. Some pictures of a couple about my own age hung on the wall. The slender man wore glasses, his arm around the waist of the woman; her hair was the same blonde as Royce's, and she had his kind eyes. They stood in front of the same mantel, and that ornament – or at least a representation of it – was behind them.

'Mistress Eva, your room is ready.' Royce carried a bundle of sheets with him as he nodded back over his shoulder.

'And you were the one saying that I shouldn't knock. You can't be calling me that if we're supposed to be together. Eva will be just fine. You called me Eva when we were younger, and it's okay to go back to it.'

He shuffled his feet a little. 'But you couldn't do magic then.'

'I can't now either! Not without Archie. For now, at least, I'm the same as everyone else in the village.'

Royce bundled the sheets into a basket and sat on the nearest chair.

Doug tried to tug the sheets back out of the basket.

'What's it like?' Royce gestured at Doug. 'How does it feel to really know what they're thinking?'

'It's a lot of food and discussion about smells. There's no guesswork about needing to relieve himself. But more than that, it's a bond like no other. I feel lost without him. I can't feel him, and there's an empty void inside me. He's just too far away and I'm worried. He hurt a lot in the last week – things weren't comfortable, and I'd been planning to ask for help from one of the others to ease his discomfort. It doesn't really work to use his own magic – we all have to support each other's familiars.'

'I wish I knew what he was thinking.'

'He's thinking your sheets smell good.' I laughed as Doug successfully managed to get a grip on the fabric, and it came out of the basket with a little more tugging.

The bedroom was small, and much like the other bits of the house, immaculate. How Royce kept the mud out, given the state I was used to seeing him in, was almost a magic of its own. From the main room came the happy noises of a tug of war, Doug howling and Royce laughing and encouraging him. It might be simple, but this was a happy house. Amy's earlier snide remarks about having to stay here came back to me. If my punishment was to have to stay in a lovely house with a sweet dog and all this good food, then I still preferred my situation to having to deal with Dotty-The-Second.

I unpacked my bag into a few empty drawers Royce had left open and flung my favourite blanket across the bed. I was still soaked – dragging mud and water across the floors would not make me a considerate guest.

As I changed, Doug's howls were replaced by music. Once dry and clean, I returned to the room to find Doug and Royce doing some ridiculous dancing. Doug wove through Royce's legs and stood on his back legs, spinning around with his paws up. I'd assumed that Satu would be the one to do the dancing familiar challenge, but watching Doug and Royce play together … maybe there was hope that Doug could do the same for me.

'You know someone has to compete in the dancing familiar contest? Satu took fastest familiar off and switched it.' I sunk into the nearest chair and watched closely. 'How are you doing that?'

'Watch my hands.' Royce gestured in motions that, as I studied them, reflected the dance Doug then did. The more I watched, the more I spotted links between his hand gestures and Doug's response to them. This dog was so clever.

'Can I try?' I stood and called Doug. He glanced up at Royce as if checking he had permission, then trotted over. I tried spinning my wrist like Royce.

Nothing happened.

Royce crossed the room. 'If I may touch your hand?'

I nodded. His hands were warm, rough from work, but his grip was soft, and he moved my wrist in a subtly different way to my first attempt.

'Spin,' he commanded, and Doug did it. 'Try again.'

I did, and this time, Doug span around just as he had before.

'If I could learn them all …'

'It would be better than asking Dusty to dance – that's for sure. We don't have long, but if you work on this with Doug, it will help his attachment to you as well.'

'We're going to need a lot of cheese and sausage.' I tried to hold back the laughter, but a giggle escaped me. I was going to compete at the Games after all!

'And time. You need to start practising. Who chooses the music?'

Doug padded over to his bed and flopped on it – although *on* would be too generous a term for the half on, half off situation he ended up in.

'We have a list of a few tunes, then they pick at random on the day.'

'As long as they all have the same speed beat, we can put together a routine. You and Doug will have to learn it.'

Royce put a record on and started up the player. 'It won't have much charge left, but if we can get a few plays from it to work something out, then that will have to do.'

The rest of our evening was a pleasant mix of dancing and music. As the cries of deer in the wood's edge split the night, Royce turned off the music.

'Every night at this time of year.' He laughed and started to gather up the cushions from the larger sofa. I'll sleep in here with Doug. Rest well, Eva.'

'Good night, Royce.'

He put the cushions where I'd been sitting, and I reached down to stroke Doug on my way past. As I closed the door, I realised he'd dropped the 'Mistress'.

Deer still called in the woods, their haunting cries filling the night as I crawled under the covers. The bed was nice enough, soft and warm, but it wasn't my bed. It was going to take a bit of time to settle and adjust. I tried to find a comfy position, eventually settling for lying on my back.

Royce and Doug moved around the other room. The door opened, presumably to let Doug out one last time before sleep.

I wondered where Archie was. Would he be warm? His old joints wouldn't cope with being outside. Surely, no one would mistreat our familiars, would they?

Between paralysing worry for Archie's wellbeing and the pillow being just a bit too flat, I struggled to sleep. I could deal with one of the issues in the morning; the other was in Cari's hands. And she still didn't have a fake familiar.

Chapter Fifteen

Morning dew exposed the webs across the field as I walked to the village with Doug at my heels. He was on a long lead so we could practise a few of the tricks Royce had taught me. Royce had been right about that, too – it was helping his willingness to accompany me. When I loosened off the lead, he remained at my side, looking up with wide eyes for the next command or treat.

My feet broke hours of work by tiny spiderlings as I headed home. Shimmering threads of web rippled in the wind like waves, the delicate weaving held in place by anchors on grass blades.

Though my initial plan for the morning was to retrieve my own pillow, I hoped Cari had some news of our familiars – or at the very least a plan.

With my pillow tucked into a bag and Doug focused on a treat in my hand, I donned my eye mask and hopped up the steps of Pigs Might Fly.

A very ragged group sat in the meeting room. Amy looked defeated as Dotty-The-Second chewed on her sleeve. Gail wiped duck poo off her skirts, and Dusty had been banished to the corner behind a makeshift fence. Milla glanced up to meet my eyes and dropped her attention to the floor almost immediately. One of her rabbits sat calmly in her lap. The village protectorate appeared haggard, and the dark circles gave away that I was far from the only one not sleeping.

'As you finally grace us with your presence this morning, I hope the tardiness is due to some great step in progress.' Cari was the only one who appeared in charge of herself, her poise and command written in every line of her body.

'Only in as much as I can almost make Doug dance,' I replied.

'How fantastic. At least that saves us losing by boredom from a rabbit ear twitching contest.' Cari's words were so pointed they could have impaled me.

'I'm sorry.' I took my seat.

'Gail was just telling us that they managed to damage the northern canyon crossing. It means everyone has to come the one way, making it easier for us to predict their arrival. We should expect them to start arriving in the next few days.'

'In that time, the spiderweb flight-rig needs testing, and the beanstalk needs a test run. The golem is the only thing I'm currently confident we can pull off. Before the first arrivals, you all need a wash and to spend some time getting these animals looking appropriately like familiars.' Cari sat. 'I have failed in all my attempts to catch a magpie, so we have one last thing to try. We need to reserve Dandelion's magic when our guests arrive to make the fake familiars appear magical, but I'm going to attempt to use him before then to open a small portal. If we're lucky, we can reclaim our familiars, or a few of them, at least.'

Pigs Might Fly made a strange shuddering.

Satu ran down the stairs and returned with a letter. 'Westwick is letting us know they're on their way and have reached Sentraal.'

'That settles it,' Cari muttered. 'We need to try now. Eva, go get Lola. Amy, bring the ingredients. We have no time to do this the other way round. The test flight will have to be tomorrow. We need to try opening a portal.'

Amy rolled her eyes. 'You mean you get your familiar back in time, while the rest of us just have to suck it up?' But she pushed herself to her feet and trotted down the stairs with Dotty-The-Second in tow.

Cari sighed. 'Do we all agree it's worth a try? With Ralph or any other familiar here, we can try to piece together where they are, then we can send a rescue party while everyone is busy here.'

She crossed her arms, staring around the room in challenge.

'Why can't you just get them all back through the portal?' Gail whined.

Cari's mouth twisted at the corner. 'If I can, then I will. But we can't risk exhausting Dandelion. He simply doesn't hold enough magic to make a portal big enough for Dotty or Jerry. We either need to use who we can rescue to make a bigger portal, or we need to send a rescue team.'

Gail lifted her duck-laden arm. 'No one is going to believe this is Sirathon. No familiar in history poops on their person. I will lead the mission.'

We'd already accepted that they weren't all coming through. I still held a thread of hope close to my heart that I could retrieve Archie, that I could see his adorable furry face.

'You'll have to leave before they get here,' Satu said. 'As soon as we have a destination for you.'

Gail nodded, and tension left her shoulders. She'd get to see Sirathon soon and know how he was. She'd have the answer we all lost sleep over. I absently stroked Doug's head as he lay next to me, nudging at the pocket where I'd hidden his snacks. Would he and Archie get on well? They'd always sniffed politely in passing, but Archie hadn't played with another dog for ages.

I left them preparing the room, clearing our seats to the edges and discussing the best direction to face the portal.

Lola sat on her porch, admiring her frozen flowers. 'Is it time to fly posts?' She laughed as I drew closer, and her door knocker blew a raspberry at me.

'No. Cari insists she wants to try opening a small portal. She's asked for you and Dandelion.'

Lola sighed. 'She'll get a portal about the size of a dinner plate – if she's lucky. I told her to wait, but she simply can't. Always impatient, that one. But then, she's your leader now, so I should do as I'm told.' Dandelion wound around her legs as she walked down the path. 'This is really going to take it out of him, you know.'

'I know.' I offered her an arm to lean on, and she tutted at me.

'I'm not that old yet – just tired of fighting against those who think they know better. Come along, Eva. Let's watch her try. If we see your pup, we'll grab him.'

In the meeting room, a circle of herbs and spell components lay on the ground. Milla arranged them while Cari stood in the centre, directing her to perfect every placement and part of the ritual. She reached inside her pocket and pulled out a magpie feather, placing it in the circle as Lola sat heavily on a chair.

'How are we doing this, then?' she asked.

'I've prepared it all. If you could just do the final step, cast the magic, and add the correct words. Reclaiming Ralph lets us expand the portal to potentially get the others through too.'

Lola walked slowly around the circle, tweaking a few small things. She paused briefly at one bunch of herbs and mushrooms; the briefest of smiles flickered across her face, and she glanced at Milla.

'Stand behind us and keep your eyes open. Remember anything and everything you see.' Cari moved from the middle as Dandelion began strolling around the rim of the circle, his languid steps belying his age. He circled twice, and on the third time, Lola began to mutter under her breath. Quietly at first, then growing louder. The spell incantation involved spirits and souls, dreams and hope. The power of the frozen gods ... Dandelion finished his final rotation, then sat at Lola's feet. Cari twitched, the tension in the room more powerful than the weak magic Dandelion had offered up for the portal.

A tiny portal, not much wider than my full handspan split the air. A swirling blue ring of frost; the chill cut through the room. A dark scar grew on the floor beneath it.

'Hold it ...' Cari said, as we all waited for something to happen. 'Ralph! Come to me.'

The portal revealed a place that was misty and green, a damp smell rolled through. I could see willow branches. A rustling noise grew louder, and Lola started to droop. Dandelion lay down, letting out a deep sigh and curling his tail around himself.

'Got you.' Lola's hand snapped through the portal, the frost curling up her arm like lace. And as it started to close, she withdrew her hands, cradling not Ralph, but Fern. The portal closed almost immediately. The rabbit shivered violently as Milla ran to collect her. From where I stood, I saw another wink and Lola's smile.

'Did anyone see Ralph? Or any other familiar?' Lola asked.

'I saw a shed and a willow,' Gail replied.

'Wetness, willows. That's got to be Mistead.' Satu sighed. 'At least it's not too far, although we just destroyed the fastest route there.'

Cari said nothing at first. She stood, staring at Milla. 'It should have called Ralph – it should have been drawn to him. His feather was in the circle.'

Milla shook a little and shrugged. 'I don't know what went wrong with the location.' She looked around at us all. 'But it's lucky that it did. Fern says that Sirathon and Ralph are tied with jesses to stop them flying home, and they're hooded. The familiars are all in a big barn, but Fern dug her way out. There's food, but Dotty is eating most of it. Jerry is getting frustrated – he's been charging at the wall for days. Archie is okay. Food comes twice a day.'

'Take a short break and we'll try again, using Fern.'

Gail leant closer. 'Anything else? I need all the clues she can give me, just in case.'

Milla shook her head. 'Not really. A man took them in, and he's the only one they saw since.'

'A man. So helpful. Typical rabbit.' Cari stomped across the meeting room.

We re-arranged ourselves, and Milla readied herself, copying phrases over and over from Lola. As she started casting, the now familiar blue ring started to appear.

Milla repeated herself, holding Ralph's feather close to the swirling frost. Then she dropped it, clasping her hands to her ears and fell to her knees. The portal closed.

'There's some shield on them. It hurts! I can't get close enough.'

Cari sighed. 'They either realised we have Fern back – or the only reason we caught her was that she'd escaped. Gail, get moving as fast as you can. Milla, you need to put that rabbit to good use. Go and help Aran with the spider silk. Eva, I need a magpie, and I need it yesterday. You two created this problem. I have a village to appease.' She stormed out.

'Always drama with that one.' Lola chuckled. 'Ever since she was a child. It's no wonder she has such a contrary familiar. If you'll permit a retired leader to offer her words of wisdom?' Lola picked up Dandelion, cradling him in her arms. 'Poor dear is exhausted. What you need to do is feed Pigs Might Fly daily. It's a major feature of Witchgorn and needs to be functional. At the moment, it can barely lift its weight or make coffee.

'Then go and sort out the spiders. There are test flights to do first, so no rush there. By all means, play with fire flight – but spend your energy on the stuff that will matter. Dotty-The-Second's lead needs to be invisible, and Dusty's genitals need to look more real. I will have to pretend I'm a full member again, so I can help with the plant growing. A sky-hook would help anchor the plant, and takes a very small amount of Dandelion's reserves.' She shifted Dandelion in her arms. 'Gail, go to see Leesa. If we're taking her fire flight away from her, we can use her expertise with explosions in another, very distracting way. See if she'll go with you?'

As Lola's calming presence washed over us, we put her plans into action.

Chapter Sixteen

We left Milla feeding Pigs Might Fly. I wiped a cobweb from Doug's ear, reminding me of that morning's beautiful webs.

'We might be able to test the post flying system early without magic, but dew will expose it in the morning. It will have to be re-hung on the day.'

Satu strode alongside me. 'Leave me to deal with that. Aran has it well in hand – I'm sure he's already thought of it. You need to get a compliant magpie.'

Gail rushed up behind us. 'Satu, how will I get them out? If they're being held well contained enough to stop them getting home on their own ...'

'I'm sure you'll find a way.' Satu reached over and patted Gail on the shoulder. 'Take the smaller lad from Leesa's farm too. I've seen him climbing through enough windows. If you can create enough distraction, he might fit through a small space to get you all in.

Gail nodded and ran in the direction of Leesa's farm with the duck still tied to her arm.

At the edge of the woods, Royce had shown me the roosts for a number of crows and magpies. Without a clear plan to catch them, I wanted to see how close we could get. The caws of birds were audible across the paddock.

Royce waved as he strolled toward us, a bucket swinging in his hand. Doug strained at the lead, and Dusty brayed to her herd as we drew closer to them.

'Didn't expect you home so soon.' He reached down to scratch Doug behind the ear.

'We tried to get them back, but all we got was the rabbit.'

Royce laughed. 'I'm sorry, but the rabbit? The one animal you had that already looked as though Milla had a true familiar?'

Satu nodded. 'It's no laughing matter, Royce. We now have to get a magpie by any means.'

He gestured over his shoulder. 'I'm betting if you look over there, you'll see they come easy enough to food. It's keeping one by your side that's the issue.'

Royce was right. At the end of the paddock, where he'd just dumped the bucket of food, the magpies were shrieking at the goats to try to reach it.

If we could catch one – now we had Fern back – we might be able to make the magpie friendly, or at least placid, for short durations at a time. I'd managed to magically befriend a robin on one occasion. It hadn't lasted very long, but then, I wasn't very experienced.

'We need a trap.' Satu tugged on Dusty's lead.

Royce pointed at the tool shed. 'If you look in the back of there, you'll see some spare wooden timber, should be arranged by size. Might be some fencing wire too. Nails on the shelf, hammer on the wall. I've got to go help down at the new house.

One last push, and it should be done today. Leave a hole small enough for a bird to get in, but too small for them to get out of with wings open. That should do the trick. He leant over and kissed me on the cheek. I'll see you later, Eva.'

I froze, uncertain what to do in response. I settled for a smile and a wave.

'You don't need to act in my presence.' Satu called after him. He waved as he jogged across the fields. 'He's a good man. Under all the mud, he'll make someone in the village a great partner. Don't ruin that for him because of your silly mistake.'

What was she suggesting? I'd done nothing inappropriate, nothing we hadn't been told to do. We were supposed to look like a couple. Anyway, Royce had had years to chase someone in the village, if that's what he'd wanted. He could make his own decisions.

I let Doug into the house – it would be easier to work without having to hold on to him – then led Satu round the back to the immaculate shed. Just as Royce suggested, a selection of wooden timbers of varied sizes leant in a corner, and a roll of wire was neatly stowed on the shelf. His organisation made it easy to find the rest of what we needed. We took everything into the goat shelter as heavy grey clouds threatened us with rain.

We measured and cut and hammered until I had blisters from wrestling the saw. It frustrated me to see them swelling. I'd been really practical before Archie had got through to me. A year or so with magic at my fingertips had made my hands soft; I wasn't going back to that once this was all over.

We cobbled together a simple box with a small hole in the top. Small wooden rods served to wrap the wire around, and with some difficulty, we nailed them to the main box frame.

We carried it to the woodland beyond the goats, who chewed their food while staring at us with curiosity.

Our trap's uneven edges made it vulnerable to being tipped. The wood had split in a multitude of places, and now resembled a hedgehog there were so many extra nails protruding, many with bent stalks from having been hit too hard.

We stabilised it with heavy stones dropped through the hole. Then I clambered back into the goat pen to try convincing them to part with some food.

That was, in retrospect, a mistake. The goats closed in. I flapped my arms at them, and the nearest let out a loud bleat.

It was Cuddles. He pawed at the ground.

Another goat tugged at my skirt, teeth grinding as it tried to remove a chunk of fabric. Dusty called loudly from the shed where we'd left her, keen to be reunited with her herd.

Cuddles lowered his head.

The impact of the collision on the muddy ground was more than sufficient to send me sliding. My feet went from under me, and I landed in a pile of steaming goat poo with the trough still in reach. Ignoring the now increasingly curious and irritated goats, I grabbed a couple of handfuls of food and struggled to my feet.

Only to be charged again.

'Try to stand up,' Satu said between peals of laughter.

'What do you think I'm doing?'

Cuddles lowered his head again, while another goat took a taste of my hair. This time, I made it to my feet and threw some of the feed away from me. It bought me enough time to run with my remaining food for the fence, with a fresh appreciation for Royce's muddiness.

I scrabbled at the fence, my feet slipping on the wood while a goat chewed my shirt. Satu tried to help me over the top, and with Dusty still bellowing from the barn, I flopped over to safety.

'Let's put that in the trap.' Satu offered her hand to help me up, and I gave her the food. 'You smell worse than Amy does. I'll leave you to get cleaned up.'

This trap had better work.

'Do you know what music we're planning to offer for the dancing?'

Satu shook her head. 'If you come to the Phoenix Feather tonight, we could see what Beth has and choose some. Would that help Doug?'

I didn't really know, but maybe we could all use a little confidence. 'Yes, it will let us teach him the routine at a particular speed, so he can look as though he is deliberately dancing to it. At least, that's how Royce explained it.'

Satu wrinkled her nose, adding to her already innumerable wrinkles. I'd not really noticed how she was aging until then. She'd always just been there, a steady hand on the village, kind and firm.

'We'll hopefully have a magpie by then too.'

I walked back to the shed with her, then they left me to tidy Royce's tools and wood away. Doug was whining at the door by the time I was done. I slipped in, trying to keep him from getting out until I could put a lead on him. Then we went out to let him relieve himself.

Sure that no one was coming, I stripped my own wet, muddy clothes off at the doorstep and carried them into the bedroom. They could be washed later.

Doug and I spent the rest of the morning practising the moves Royce had taught me. Doug was already familiar with them; it was just me – and his desire to do them for me – where we lacked.

My hands were slick with drool and grease by the time we stopped. Doug was sort of weaving through my legs and happily spinning on his back paws to my command. It wasn't much, but as I sat down to rest, he curled up at my feet.

That was how Royce found us. I was unwilling to move while Doug snored gently.

'Some guard dog,' Royce said. He reached over me to stroke Doug.

At his touch, Doug exploded into a wagging, wiggling mass of fluff.

'Sit.' Doug sat. 'You've got a bird in that trap.'

Royce was right. There were, in fact, two birds – a magpie and a crow, cawing with palpable distress. In the branches of a nearby tree, another magpie called back. I reached my hand inside to see if I could get hold of either bird. I flailed ineffectively, and they fluttered easily out of reach.

It was at this point that our second mistake of the morning was apparent. I'd left no way, aside from cutting the wire – to get the captured birds out, and certainly not when they were this hysterical.

Royce and Doug walked over.

'It's a good trap,' he said. How were you planning to tame the magpie?

I shrugged. 'Feed it more?'

'You don't have time. There was a runner. The first visitors just tried the upper bridge. By the time they take the long way round, they should arrive tomorrow night.'

'Is everything ready?'

'I'm sure you want me to say yes, but in truth, no. The fencepost test flight went well – Aran has done an amazing job. There's still a team digging out the hole for the plant growing. If they work through the night, it should be ready.'

'The golem team are the same people doing the rest of the physical work. They need to rest before they spend the week in that contraption. Then there's you and Doug. We need to work out a routine that you can pull off.'

Cari had one day to bond with a wild magpie, and I had to learn a dance.

'I'll get the music options tonight if I go and see Beth.' I could always eat at the Phoenix Feather. It would be less of an imposition on Royce that way.

'I'll start working out a routine. How long does it have to be?'

'A few minutes, I suppose. It's been a few years since this challenge was chosen.' Royce flung his arms wide and twirled as Doug joined him, spinning around on his hind legs. 'Leave this to us. I'll have something ready for you.'

The Phoenix Feather was packed. A group of musicians warmed up on the small stage as I entered.

Beth gestured me over. 'These spiders and flies are driving me crazy, but we don't have long now. I've got the selection of music we can play over here. Satu said you'd be stopping by for a listen.'

'As long as they're all the same speed, I think it will be okay.'

I'd been trying to feed the stupid magpie all afternoon, and it still pecked my hand every time I put it through the bars. Cuts decorated my knuckles like a bloody lace glove.

'You know they'll be here tomorrow?' Beth said, nodding at my hand.

I sighed. 'I'd heard.'

Milla and Fern pushed through the gathering crowd in front of the stage. She looked exhausted. 'Cari has drained me, but we're almost ready. What happened to your hand?'

'Magpie.' Beth had slipped away. That was a shame; I could really have used a drink. Instead, I had a pile of recordings.

Milla glanced at them and sighed. 'I'll need to add some power to that, too, before we need it.' She stroked Fern's long ears. 'I'm glad to have her back, but I think maybe I hadn't thought everything through.'

I leant in close. 'How did you do it?'

'I added some of Fern's fur to the circle too.' Milla blushed. 'I know I shouldn't have, and your hands wouldn't be in that state if Ralph had appeared instead.' I reached to stroke Fern.

'In your position, with that opportunity, I can't say that I wouldn't have done the same.'

Milla raised a hand to catch Lola's attention as she wandered into the room.

'Your hands are a mess.' Lola frowned. 'Tell me why you're trying to catch the magpie?'

'For Cari.'

'I know that. I meant why not get Milla to cast friendship on it? It will need doing each day, but it's a lot easier than bribing a wild bird.'

Milla pointed at Fern. 'She has nothing left to give today.'

'Then Mistress Cari will simply have to wait until morning,' Lola retorted.

Chapter Seventeen

T hin morning light struggled through the white curtains and dusty windows. Today was the day. Fern and Dandelion had a lot to achieve, and I hoped we could pull it off. Behind the worry of being caught out loomed the bigger, darker concern. I couldn't get Gail's rescue mission out of my head. If she was successful, I suppose we'd see Sirathon or Ralph return before her, but so would whoever had taken them all. It would be a long walk for a small, elderly dog.

My worry for Archie must have shown over breakfast. As we sat on the porch, enjoying the peace of the day, Royce reached across the table and put his hand on mine, giving it a gentle squeeze.

'He'll be alright, you'll see.'

I hoped he was right. Somehow, I had to get through the next few days. The other members of the village protectorate must share my concerns. Amy struggled outwardly, but the rest must be feeling every bit as incomplete as me – if not more so for the older members. I'd been used to functioning without magic, but they were much further removed from that independence than I was. I reached to scratch Doug's ear, his soft fur similar to Archie's, curls wrapped around my finger.

'I'm sure he will. Gail will get them back.'

Cari's voice broke our peace, preceding her appearance around the side of the house. 'Eva Eclipse, I hear you have a magpie for me.'

I fixed a smile on my face and took one last gulp of coffee before I answered.

'I do. Shall I show you?'

Cari was followed by a fraught-looking Milla and Fern. 'How's the dancing going?' she asked.

'Slowly.'

'Don't listen to her – they're doing brilliantly,' Royce replied.

I hoped his faith in us paid off. 'The birds are over here.'

I led them to the cage which now held three birds. The magpie's partner had stopped calling from the trees at some point in the night, so I suspected we had them both.

Cari crouched by the cage, and for the first time in days, I saw a small drop in the tension of her shoulders.

'That one.' She pointed at the bigger of the two. 'How do we get them out?'

'I'll have to cut the wire.'

'Let me cast friendship first.' Milla sat as close to the trap as she could get, cradling Fern in her lap. She closed her eyes and stroked the rabbit for a few moments.

We all asked our familiars for help differently, and I was used to her silences. Once she was ready, her fingers wiggled, Fern's nose twitched, and a slight glow formed into an elongated, rippling, golden thread. Cari clasped her hand around one end of it, while Milla manipulated the other to make contact with the magpie. She closed her fingers to make a fist, and the glow disappeared.

The magpie turned to face Cari, cocked its head to one side, and cawed. She reached out to offer it something. The bird hopped closer, reaching through the wire to take a seed from her outstretched hand.

'Well done. Cut him free, please.'

I ran back toward the tool shed, but Royce met me halfway. 'You'll be needing these.' He handed me the wire cutters. 'Leave it where it is, just in case.'

I rushed back and carefully cut a large hole. The magpie hopped onto Cari's arm as though he were a true familiar, while the crow flapped away into the woods, followed by the second magpie. It alighted on a branch overlooking the paddock, watching us closely.

'I don't expect to see you in the village until the sun sets, Eva. The first protectorates are due to reach us about then. Once you've greeted each party with us, you are relieved of all other magical responsibilities aside from dancing and pretending to be a couple. I am sorry for the inconvenience, Royce.' She directed the last past my shoulder.

Royce stood behind me. 'Mistress Cari, I'll ensure Doug is a good dog throughout.'

'Please do. Milla needs to preserve her energy to keep Pigs Might Fly working, and Dandelion is maintaining illusions on the other familiars. This is a well-trained animal. I'm sure you can make this work.' With that, she turned and walked away.

Milla rushed over and reached for my arms. A gentle pulse of healing flowed through the scars, and the itching faded. I pulled my sleeve back to reveal natural, smooth skin.

'I have to go, sorry!' Milla whispered, before scurrying after Cari.

We strolled back to the house with Doug running ahead, looking back occasionally or sniffing at some wonderful – to him – smell.

'Well-trained animal! She should see him when it's dinner time.' Royce opened the door for me, giving a deep bow. 'Would you care to dance, Mistress Eva?'

'Inside? I'll have to do it in a field with all the distractions in a few days' time.'

He nodded. 'Start inside, we can move out later. You don't want them to see you practising if this is supposed to look magical and spontaneous. We can dance in the paddock if you really want a challenge – once you've learnt a sequence of moves.'

My last mud-covered visit to the goat paddock didn't inspire me with confidence. At least a field of spectators wouldn't try to push me over, although I wouldn't put it past Dusty.

Royce pushed the furniture back to the edges of the room, the floor beneath as clean and pristine as everywhere else in the house. With some space made, he called Doug to him.

'Start with asking him to stand.'

Doug rose up on his back legs, paws to either side of his head and, at a gesture from Royce, span around. 'He will watch your body. You need to mirror what I do.'

I stood up and tried to mimic his movement. Royce frowned. 'Hmm ... it's similar, but not quite right. May I move you into position?'

I nodded.

His hands were gentle, but firm, moving my hand in a precise pattern, my shoulders to an exact pose. He was so close I could feel his breath on my neck.

'Okay, try that again,' he said.

I called Doug and tried to move as Royce had shown me. This time, Doug rose to his feet, span, and then sat facing me.

'Well done! Both of you.' He slipped a treat into my hand, and I passed it forward to Doug. 'Next, we need to incorporate that leg weave you've been trying.'

Royce repeated the first steps again, adding in a complex route for Doug to run around and between his legs. They were clearly adept at this, and Doug's tail wagged so hard as he played that I thought he might take off. Faster and faster they went until, eventually, Doug started barking and Royce folded double with laughter.

'Maybe I should start that a little slower,' I said. Royce turned, pushing his glasses back into place.

'I'm not sure you ever need to go that fast. Doug was enjoying it, and I got a little carried away.' He stood and brushed dog hairs from his trousers. I caught a glance at a broom in the corner, but then he switched his attention back to me. 'The biggest issue we have, really, is those skirts.'

He was right. If I wanted to do that weaving move, I needed to find something else to wear. I used to wear trousers before I joined the village protectorate. I suppose I'd become used to this traditional dress since.

'I don't have trousers any more. I do in my house possibly, but not here.'

'We don't have time for you to go home, and it's not worth upsetting Mistress Cari. Wait there.' As if I was going anywhere else. Royce went into the bedroom and returned with a pair of his trousers. They were cut slightly loose, and he had a belt hung over his arm. 'They may be a little big, but you can always use this. No one will see you in here.'

I took them. The fabric was stiff and quite rough, but they looked as though they might fit reasonably well. 'I'll get them on – just give me a moment.'

As I changed, Royce called through the door. 'Does Larent have your measurements?'

'Is there anyone in town whose measurements he doesn't have?' I opened the door, and he looked at the fit appraisingly. 'Turn around.' I felt exposed as he studied me. 'They don't look like yours – they don't even look like you'd have chosen to borrow them from me.' He laughed. 'I've seen sacks gathered looser. Let me teach you the new steps, then I'll visit Larent for you and see what he can dream up. The beanstalk is fully made. What remains is purely digging and Beth's chemicals.'

He spent a while positioning me again, gently helping me move through the sequence of steps to get Doug to copy me. Side by side we danced, and in front of us, Doug responded to the cues.

'How on earth did you discover Doug danced?' I asked as the dog span on his hind legs again.

'We've had a lot of winter evenings alone out here,' Royce replied. 'Some of it was practical, for herding the goats, then we got carried away adding more tricks.' He knelt and did a small gesture with his right hand. Doug ran behind him, jumped onto his back, then sprung off, twisting to land on his feet.

'Never really thought we'd be showing anyone else these.' He bent over to scratch Doug.

'When Archie gets back, do you think you can show me how to teach him too?'

Royce nodded. 'You'd best get practising. I'll see what Larent can stitch up for you.'

Chapter Eighteen

My new split skirts swished as I walked; whatever fabric Larent had made them from was more fluid than I'd usually wear, but it was what I had to work with. I wasn't too unhappy with how it flattered me. And, if I was honest, I felt good in them. It was unconventional, but let me move, and Doug was able to dance around them with ease.

After a full day of dancing, I was exhausted, but determined not to let the rest of the protectorate down – again. As long as the dancing familiar challenge wasn't on day one, we could do this.

The other pay-off from all the training was that, to my delight, Doug now walked calmly by my side, off the lead. The specially lined pocket in my new trousers was filled with treats and aided his commitment to good behaviour. I'd no idea how Larent had done it, but I no longer wafted around in a cloud of sausage and cheese.

The heavy footfall of our golem broke my daydreaming as I strode across the field toward where I'd last seen Pigs Might Fly. Inside that stone body, a bunch of teenagers pulled on ropes and sweated profusely. I hoped they were well supplied with cookies and water, and they'd fixed the visibility issue. I watched them roam, and although Amy stood in full view of the golem, it appeared to be negotiating the field without her shouting anything at it. That was a relief.

I brushed the mask across my eyes to find the steps as subtly as possible. Pigs Might Fly had returned to wandering around its field, much to my relief and the locals' frustration. Without enough of us to recharge masks, it was possible to find the building by seeing who just rebounded from the wall.

My foot landed solidly on the first step, so I continued on up. Pigs Might Fly opened the door, and I entered to the scent of fresh coffee and cookies. Milla stood by the counter, beaming.

'So far, so good,' she whispered.

The magpie sat calmly on Cari's arm, Dandelion snored fitfully, and even Dusty appeared a little less agitated.

'How's the dancing?' Cari asked. 'Can you pull it off?' She looked at the way Doug followed me and nodded. 'That's much better.'

'We need another day, if I'm honest. But I think we can just about do it. The only thing is, I'll have to dance too.'

Satu shrugged. 'You're new and enthusiastic. I'm sure we can all agree on that. Amy will be doing the golem race and Milla the fire-flight. Lola will grow the plant, you're dancing, and either myself or Cari will pretend to race the fencepost. Most of the other protectorates would expect me to be based in here – after all, I always am.'

It would restrict Dusty from causing too much trouble, or being studied in brighter light. I could see the sense in the plan.

Pigs Might Fly turned, and our new view exposed a group of people in the distance with a pair of golems towering above them.

'It's time.' Lola nudged Dandelion awake. 'Just an hour or so, old man, then we can go home and hide.'

We left Pigs Might Fly together. Milla and Amy joined as we walked to the main village gate, our golem following ponderously behind. Its slight pauses as the GPS adjusted the balance were noticeable, but then I expected it – was looking for it. Hopefully, to someone expecting a golem to be a golem and not eight sweaty teenagers in a stone suit, it would look relatively normal.

We were greeted by a trio of individuals leading a larger group of travellers. I recognised one as the leader of Sentraal, Berta Kimura. She was quick witted, and her snake familiar wound its way up her arm like a bracelet. It made me nervous. I hadn't really thought about how the other familiars might perceive our familiars – I hoped Cari had considered it.

'What a pleasure to be visiting your protectorate, Cari Elphic,' she said as she stepped forward.

'Thank you for giving us notice, Berta. We've prepared a site for your tents, away from the noise of the village.' Cari bowed deeply to the old man and woman heading up the other protectorates. They were more of an age with Satu, and barely younger than Lola.

'I thought you were stepping back?' the woman said as she saw Lola.

'One small step at a time.' Lola gestured at Cari. 'I have stepped quite a long way back, just not entirely away, yet. It's good to see you, Adela. Where's the Westwick Golem? I can't help but notice that you've only brought two golems between your three protectorates.'

The older woman nodded. 'I think it's fair to say, as we are amongst friends here in the South, that things have been getting a little tense recently. We've made the decision to forfeit the race, but leave one of our newer recruits in charge of the West-wick golem. It's strategically positioned on the route into Sentraal village.'

If they'd made a decision to risk a forfeit, things across Two Chasms must be worse than we'd realised. Maybe the other tensions would be sufficient to make our own problem less apparent.

Dandelion purred as he approached Adela, rubbing against her legs for attention. Dusty pawed at the ground and Satu sighed. 'Some of them just don't mellow with age like that one. I'll let Milla and Eva show you to your site. Feel free to join us in Pigs Might Fly once your tents are up.

The man shuddered as he looked past us. 'That thing always makes me travel sick. Did you know the north bridge is out?'

'I'll get someone right on it – I'm sure it will be repaired by the time you head home. As you're here to witness it, we could do the choosing ceremony this evening at the Phoenix Feather?'

He nodded. 'It's acceptable once at least three villages are gathered. I'd not mind having an extra day's warning over Raventor or Seastone Keep. We need every advantage we can get.' He turned to me. 'Talking of advantages, I understand that you're the newest member of the protectorate. It's a pleasure to meet you, Eva Eclipse. Toby Dogwood of Chasmdeep at your service.' The man held his hand out, and I shook it uncertainly.

'Thank you. It's been quite an experience so far.'

We led them up the hill, with Doug mostly behaving. As long as I kept putting my hand into the pocket, he trotted by my side perfectly. We crested the hill to the familiar grazing paddock where one of our own travel tents had been erected over the portal scar. Mathilda bustled around inside, setting out tables and seats for our guests.

'Did you, umm ...' How could I ask Milla about Mathilda's bruise in front of the other protectorates? It would sound odd if we asked each other about a routine task.

Milla stroked Fern. 'Yes, I helped her out.'

'You'll have to show me how you do it one day.' I kept my eyes on Mathilda, and sure enough, when she turned to greet us, the bruise was gone. She waved cheerfully.

'Will we all be in the one field?' Berta asked.

'No, Raventor will be out in that field, as they always prefer the cooler shade of trees.' I pointed at Leesa's farm and the small copse of trees where it bordered the paddock. 'Mistead will be here, too, on the other side of the field.'

'And no doubt Seastone Keep will stay in the Phoenix Feather. Too proud and fancy to sleep anywhere outdoors.' She sniffed and gestured for their golem to move forward with the huge bundle it carried.

Both golems were soon relieved of their burden, and we left them to put their tents up and settle in.

Milla looked worried as we returned to Pigs Might Fly. 'I don't like the sound of that,' she murmured. 'No one forfeits a race.'

'I'm more worried that their golem might end up getting in Gail's way, or they think we're involved in whatever they're dealing with by sending her away at this time.'

'We have to trust in our plan. There's nothing else we can do now.' Milla put Fern down and let her hop alongside us. 'Hopefully, we get a little bit of luck with the event order. I'd like an extra day or so for the fire flight. Not that I can practise much. Once I've fed Pigs Might Fly, reinforced Cari's friendship, and hidden Dusty's lead, I'm not exactly fizzing with magic.' As we strolled companionably down the hill, the setting sun turned the sky a symphony of red, orange, and pink, with notes of purple at the edges.

Amy waved at us – beckoning us to hurry – and reluctantly, I picked up my pace. Doug trotted a little faster, less time for sniffing the grass or trying to pounce on occasional small birds. I worried that being stricter and pulling away from the things that he wanted to do would push him away, but so far, he'd continued to accept my leadership.

Amy and Dotty-The-Second ran toward us.

'Raventor, we think, and Mistead are here now.'

This was it. If our hunch was right, Mistead had our familiars, and we couldn't say a word without giving ourselves away. But if they were trying to instigate something bigger than some small inconvenience to us, it was even more important we pulled this off.

Chapter Nineteen

Phoenix Feather was more packed than the inside of our golem, and, I suspected, just as sweaty. It was an excellent move by Cari. People were so packed in that having any opportunity to really inspect our familiars would be impossible, unless we stood them next to another protectorate. Royce stuck close to me, Doug positioned between us, so he didn't get stood on. As more and more people pushed in, he gestured to a table.

I tried to slip through the crowd, but the last time I'd been in a crowd this dense, I was younger and slimmer. Now it was more challenging to shove my way past. Doug disappeared under the table as we sat down, his paws safe from trampling – for a while at least.

Beth waved from the bar, and Aran stood near the stage. He looked tired. I hadn't seen him much in the last few days, and the carefree young man, who liked magic and played sleight of hand, was barely there.

Beth spent entirely too much time glancing down near her feet. The spiders must still be under the bar. The only one of the group who'd pulled the villagers together, with any enthusiasm left, was Larent. He waved cheerily at me and slipped through the crowd far more easily than I did.

'Do you like them?' he asked.

'I love them. Whatever you've done with this pocket has stopped all the smell.'

He leant in close. 'It's a scrap from the lining of my big project. That fabric doesn't leak, which is why you can't smell anything.' He stood and looked around at the protectorates.

'Do you think it's worth me sewing up a few more? It's about time you updated your dress code anyway.'

Royce nodded. 'It's entirely impractical. First, there's the amount of washing, then the mud, and those skirts are entirely incompatible with feeding the goats.'

A protectorate member close to us turned around slightly as we talked. Royce's voice was carrying louder than he had maybe intended.

I put my hand on his. It felt strange trying to show public affection, though not unpleasant. His hand was warm under mine. 'No one needs to know about my washing. But I do think that these split skirts would be wonderfully practical for other protectorate members, if their rules bend far enough to accommodate them. Our situation was a little different, remember?'

Royce blushed as he looked down at our hands. Larent raised an eyebrow in question.

'Of course. Maybe I'll make a few pairs anyway. Even though I'd rather make them to order – they look far more flattering made to measure.'

As we chatted, the door opened, and a group of men in black outfits tried to stride in, their dramatic entrance diffused by sheer numbers. Few people noticed them; most of the crowd watched the stage, where Cari and her magpie ascended the steps with the other leaders close behind.

'We're here now. You can start,' their apparent leader called out. Cari snorted so loudly that I thought it was Dusty.

'You'd better come and join us then,' she replied.

He hustled to the front, and as the last one, he ended up squeezed against the wall.

'Let us draw for the events of day one.' Cari reached into a covered basket and pulled out a small box. 'Event one, morning, to be chosen by … Raventor,' she called out, loudly enough that I suspected the spiders under our feet heard her.

Their representative took the block and placed it on the table. 'Raventor chooses the golem race. Three laps of the cafe field.'

Three laps! Our poor GPS. They'd be exhausted. Lola patted a slightly stressed looking Paulie, but Aran didn't respond at all. He remained calm and relaxed, leaning against the inn wall.

What we really needed was the growing and the fencepost race on different days.

Cari passed the basket to her left. The Raventor representative reached in and rummaged around before withdrawing the block. 'Event two is chosen by … Chasmdeep.'

Toby Dogwood reached for the cube. 'Chasmdeep chooses fencepost racing.' He went in for the next block. 'Mistead.'

A wet-looking woman slouched her way to the front to take the cube. I had never seen someone so dry who managed to portray the essence of the misery I felt when entirely soaked to the skin. Her hair hung in straight curtains past her face, her clothes were heavy and clung to her. She turned to Cari and smiled. It was predatory, a hunter about to attack.

'Mistead chooses fire-flight, and that means it is on the first night.'

Cari's face remained an immovable mask. 'Thank you. I've no doubt it will be a spectacle – as ever.'

Milla didn't have the extra time she'd hoped for. It also meant that my event was definitely the second day, as was the beanstalk growing. Aside from the fire flight we'd now given to Milla, beanstalk was the one most likely to go wrong.

I trusted Larent more now I'd experienced these pockets, but still, there were so many things that might not work.

As the game draw came to a close, I took a long swig of my drink.

'We need to get through three days. Just three days,' I murmured.

Royce leant in close. 'We have three more nights. You and Doug can do this.'

Three more nights in his house. Hopefully three or less days until Archie was on his way back, and I could return to my normal life. Milla squeezed through the crowd.

'He's here,' she hissed. 'I don't think he's seen me yet, but he's here.'

'He who?' Larent asked.

I saw him then. 'The cow-eyed boy. The reason she wasn't with me when things went wrong.'

He moved through the crowd as though searching for someone. Trying to get close to our protectorate.

'That one.' I pointed at him as subtly as I could manage.

Larent eyed him. 'Leave him to me,' he declared. 'He's wearing fine fabric. I can distract him well enough.'

'Not too well that he gives himself away, I hope,' Royce muttered as Larent made a direct line for the man. It was time for us to make a swift exit. He'd recognise me, and the less time he saw me with Doug, the better.

'Won't he wonder how you have Fern back if she is supposed to be captive in Mistead? You should lay low – stick to your jobs, and don't do anything showy.' I looked at her more closely. 'Cari is going to go mad when she realises you've been wasting magic on makeup.'

'Cari can dance on my wand,' she whispered. 'It makes my mother happy. That's the key thing. She's willing to leave the house and deliver her cookies with her makeup done. It's silly, I know, and I hope I don't end up regretting it.'

'They're going to expect you to mess up at some point,' Royce said, leaning in close to us. 'What you need to do is make it through for long enough that Gail can free the rest. Just trust us. Witchgorn has got your back.'

'I know – you've all been amazing. I'm worried about the GPS, though. It's asking a lot from them.'

'We were all young with boundless energy and working joints once upon a time,' Royce said. 'They'll talk about this for the rest of their lives.'

He was right, but I'd been inside it. They would be aching and tired. 'We can't restart the golem until all the mechanisms are removed, even if the others get back – they have to carry on to the end.'

'I'm telling you, don't worry. They feel part of something. Maybe less of them will leave for Seastone Town or Nevsern than usual as they start looking for work. It would be good to keep more of them around.'

He was right. If we could pull this off, then maybe we'd have created a new dynamic in the village. We could make more use of the skills everyone else had. No longer be the backwood little village, but a link between Two Chasms folk and the non-magikers of Nevsern – a place where many of our younger folk felt valued. I wasn't long enough out of being normal that I'd forgotten the frustration of having to ask for help.

'Milla, can you spare a little extra top-up now?' Royce pulled his mask from his pocket. 'I can always use mine to get

Eva to Pigs Might Fly. She can't be looking for it through a mask. We'll stand out more than enough as it is.'

Milla winked and put the mask under Fern. A few moments later, she returned a now fluff-covered mask beneath the table.

'Has he gone yet?' she asked.

Larent had cornered the cow-eyed man with animated and excited talk. They appeared to be deep in conversation. Each time he tried to step away, Larent would start talking again.

'I think you'd better sneak out the bar door,' I replied. Milla got up and, holding Fern against her chest, worked her way casually to the bar. Beth leant in close, then Milla slipped past her into the kitchen and was gone.

'That's one encounter. She can't avoid him for the whole three days.' Royce frowned as she went. Doug had started to nibble my shoe under the table, so I reached down to stroke him.

'Time to go home ourselves,' I said. 'Before Doug outs himself.'

Royce stood. 'May I put my arm around you to escort you out?' he asked. 'It's a closely packed room. I feel it would look more natural.'

I nodded.

We left the inn, our bodies closer than they had been since ... well, since ever. I couldn't even recall a moment in childhood where we'd hugged. Yet, it didn't feel as uncomfortable as I'd expected. In fact, it was rather nice, and I felt the lack of his proximity once we were out of sight and he stepped away.

Chapter Twenty

After our morning dance practise, Doug, Royce, and I took a stroll into the village. Tents dotted the far hill, with people bustling around between them and a steady trickle going into Mathilda's tent for food.

'There's a flyer.' I pointed at a post of wood whizzing over the trees.

'Lucky there are no rules for height,' Royce said, craning his head back as a burst of light exploded silently over our heads. It was beautiful, and at night, it would have been stunning. But I couldn't help worrying that Milla had no spare magic to practise.

It didn't matter. We only had to look as though we were competing, not win the events. All we had to do was appear to still hold enough power, that this town wasn't ready to be swallowed up – to become another satellite of Seastone Keep like Nevsern, all their magic taken to the keep, and a town left reliant on the protection from afar, with tithes they could not easily meet.

Milla was doing all the things we needed, re-enforcing

bonds, feeding Pig-Might-Fly, hiding leads and collars from sight, and softening the attachment lines of fake male anatomy on Dusty. To me, the air crackled with magic so intensely that we might be lucky, and the lack of contribution from our protectorate might go unnoticed.

We were due in Pigs Might Fly for the official presentation of competitors at midday. Once this was done, there was no going back.

Royce led me to the steps. Coffee assaulted my nose as I entered, and the chocolatey smell of freshly baked cookies had my mouth watering. Royce made a direct line for the bar with a sparkle in his eye.

'I've always wanted to try the machine. As I'm officially a spare part of the protectorate this week, can I?'

Satu laughed. Behind her, in the depths of the kitchen area, Dusty pawed at the ground. She was behaving no better, then. At least she was semi-hidden, and as she moved around, her *additions* appeared natural, so whatever Milla and Fern had put in place for the illusion was working. Dusty and Dotty remained our weakest links. Dotty-The-Second was out in full view of everyone, and in sight of the golem. They normally required a line-of-sight operator for active walking, rather than guarding, so it was the best we could do to keep her from scrutiny.

Satu gestured Royce to join her. 'You put the water in here. Then the coffee in there.' She pulled open a compartment.

Royce peered in, then scooped coffee to fill it up. 'How do I work it?'

'Much like your cool box, you just press the button. The stored magic will trickle into it from Pigs Might Fly's reserves, and…' She stepped back as the machine started to make a noise.

'I've got it.' Royce's face lit up. 'This smells a lot better than what I usually have to deal with. I can carry on if it frees you to host our guests?'

Aran arrived next, escorting one of the GPS team, who sported a big, visible bruise on their face. 'Can you help?' he called as they appeared at the doorway. He glanced back over his shoulder as Satu and I stared at him.

'You know we can't! Aran, what are you doing?'

Aran chuckled and quickly took a cloth from his pocket. 'Water, quick!' he said.

Royce passed him some water. They dunked the cloth, and I suspect I looked a little like a startled fish as the entire bruise wiped off the teenager's face, along with whatever they had made the swelling with.

'Thank you, Mistress Satu,' they said very loudly as they turned to leave, while trying to hide the laughter in their voice. They exited almost as swiftly as they appeared, leaving us in stunned silence as Royce burst into a loud belly laugh.

Moments after they must have reached the base of the steps, the door opened, and Berta appeared at the doorway.

'I do love that your village is so open about sharing this place with the rest of the residents,' she said, glancing after them. 'I wish ours were as relaxed. We live at one end of the village while they hide behind us, only visiting for help.'

Satu offered her a coffee. 'Maybe being more isolated means we have to work together more. Cookie? They're made by Milla Russet's mother, and while non-magical, they come as close as it's possible to get without a little enhancement.'

'More co-operation.' Berta took the coffee and cookie, then settled into a cosy chair. She looked up at Royce. 'You're no magiker that I know?'

I could feel my hands sweat a little, but I trusted him. I'd not jump in.

'No, I'm Eva Eclipse's companion.'

Berta raised an eyebrow. 'Most unusual, although, so was Eva, being such a late bloomer. We can't expect everyone to stay celibate just in case. It must have been quite the shock to discover you were with a magiker.'

He smiled broadly and pushed his glasses up his nose as he looked at me. 'It really was. Not an unpleasant surprise, though, I have to say.'

Berta's scrutiny switched to me, her eyes widening as she took in my split skirts.

'How modern,' she gasped. 'I'm surprised Cari Elphick allowed such a change. She's always struck me as a traditionalist.'

Cari appeared at the bottom of the stairs, the magpie sat comfortably on her shoulder as she fed it a nut.

'Really, Berta? I suppose things change with need and time. Like the wind howling through the canyons, we must move forward or get stuck in an eddy of our own making.' To my utter shock, she wore skirts like mine, the fabric almost shimmering with the colours of a magpie in sunlight.

'Would you like to come up? I saw the others approaching from the window. We can't fit everyone up there, so leaders only, I'm afraid. It's a bit too cosy for us all.'

Berta took another cookie on her way past, glancing at Dusty. 'Jerry looks like he's been eating well. You might want to let him have a shot at some siring soon. More goat familiars would be fantastic – I'd certainly like some in Sentraal. They're more intimidating than smaller creatures.' Her snake's head peered out at me from inside her sleeve as she left the room to follow Cari.

Others soon arrived. The black-clad leader of Seastone Keep didn't spare us a glance, nor the others, as they arrived and we directed them upstairs. The lanky-haired woman from Mistead narrowed her eyes at me, then slouched past with her frog in close pursuit to study the fireplace.

'This is functional?' she asked.

'Of course. Did you need to send a message?'

She paused, looking around. Doug peered out from between Royce's feet. Dusty bleated from the kitchen. As Dusty started again, Royce pressed the button on the coffee brewer, and it hissed and hummed while it made more coffee. I had honestly no idea what we would do with so much of it. But it distracted the woman from the fire.

'Interesting,' she murmured as the fizz of magic filled the air with the scent of coffee, right above Doug's head. 'I may avail myself of the system later. It is crude and far less elegant than a flying letter.'

'But much more efficient in the rain,' Satu replied quickly. 'I believe they're waiting on you up there, Cora.'

'Let them wait. Nothing starts until tomorrow. Tell me, Eva Eclipse, which talent will you be exhibiting for your first Games?'

'I'll be doing dancing familiar.' I looked over at Doug, and at my words, Royce had made the gesture we'd used to tell Doug to spin on his hind legs. Doug was doing just that. He was such a good dog.

'I hope, for your sake, you are better at that than you are at catching ducks.' With that, she smiled and started to climb the stairs. 'By the way, where *is* Gail? This village is in such a useful location, and has so much room to expand.' She didn't wait for a response.

'Well, that confirms it.' Satu positively bristled.

Chapter Twenty-One

Overnight, Milla and Satu coaxed Pigs Might Fly into a central position. The cafe wasn't known for its willing cooperation, so there was still a chance it would get involved in the race or move into the way. Both issues Amy would be completely unable to do anything about, or even see.

Amy stood tall and proud as the golems lined up. At least outwardly, that's how she appeared. The Amy I knew, snide and confident, stood in the competition space, not the frustrated one who'd skulked around the village for the last couple of weeks. She and the pig sat within their circle, watching our golem get into position as though nothing was a problem in the slightest.

Each protectorate competitor was not allowed to step outside their own circle, to restrict the possibility of interference in each other's space. It wasn't used all the time – it was considered an extra challenge to maintain control from a distance – but Raventor had insisted. We were happy to oblige. It significantly reduced the chance Dotty-The-Second would be in close proximity to any other familiar.

Golems lumbered toward the start line, staggered as the closest golem had a shorter route. On the second lap, they would all race around the outer edge of the field, and the same for the third. Aran and a group of others stood near the start, ready to throw a finishing line up once the laps had begun.

The purple prepare flag was lifted by Paulie.

All golems moved slightly – this was the point they would be receiving their instruction. Ours copied, badly. A shudder-like motion rattled it as they lined up to go. With none of the usual golem stability, it swayed slightly.

The green flag raised and dropped, and the ground shook as the group lumbered forward.

Our golem took a while to get underway, one slightly unstable step after another as they tried to keep up with golems self-aware of their own body. The eight teenagers in a rock suit were doing brilliantly, though. Whoever had the direction mirror was keeping them clear of collisions. They were last to the first corner, but they made it round in one piece, all the practise of the last week paying off. As they straightened up for the next side of the field, our golem's arms flung wide for balance, almost colliding with another racer. For a moment, I thought I'd heard a squeal from it, but some young child near the fence let out another shout as they passed. Maybe it was just a spectator.

As long as the other protectorates thought the same.

The lumbering golems passed me. The leader, a slick, light-weight golem from Seastone Keep, looked almost human, leaving the more traditional goliaths far in its wake. No one would ever expect us to win. Ours was the tallest of the chasing pack. We just had to not collapse or expose the hollow middle and the sweaty teenagers powering it.

All eyes were on the race, watching as the golems finished

their first lap. The protectorate golem drivers in their circles all looked fresh, no one struggled yet.

Amy followed ours with her body, turning to keep herself aligned as it ran. They passed Aran in an earth-shuddering sprint for position as they had to return to the outer track. No one wanted to be stuck in a position their golem would find it hard to pull past the others from.

The leading golem had stopped.

Everyone turned to stare at it. What was Seastone doing? They had a lead. The young protectorate member had lost focus, busy gazing at the rest of the pack.

'Ross!'

The young man shook his hedgehog familiar awake, his attention returned to his golem, and it started running.

'That helped Aran.' Royce chuckled.

Aran had sent some of his group off as the events unfolded, and they had reached the edge of the woods. The spider silk rigging had been tested and retested. I knew they could set it up in a matter of minutes if they were all in place.

A golem tripped, and the rest had to navigate past it. I held my breath as the GPS negotiated the danger safely. Aran's team used the change to pass the thread back; a subtle motion, a hooking of one part onto another. The tiny transparent rings threaded into place.

I didn't know if Satu would risk Dusty or if Cari had decided to try the magpie. But either way, the familiar would be attached to the post, pulling it with them as they raced to the wood and back again.

A clattering of stone drew my focus back to the race. The second lap was halfway done, and our golem was looking tired. I hadn't known it was possible for a stone golem to look tired, but it did. Amy was sagging slightly, putting her acting and dramatic skills to good use. It looked as though they might overbalance at the last corner, and they hit another golem ... again. If they weren't careful, they'd get a retaliatory wallop, and at this stage, I didn't know if they'd have enough control to stay upright.

'Witchgorn, Witchgorn.' A quiet chant grew from the spectating members of the GPS on their break. It was highly unusual to cheer on any event at the inter-village Games, given it might impact the magiker's concentration, but the villagers didn't care. In their sweaty rock suit, our golem heard. They picked the pace up, and Amy responded to them too. The teenagers at the rail edge cheered as *their* golem ran past.

This whole event was unconventional, I supposed. Royce soon joined the chant, spurring the GPS on into their third and final circuit. Before long, the chant was picked up by others in the village, and slowly, the rail-side GPS drifted away in ones and twos back to their grow-your-muscles club. When I had my magic back, I'd have to find a way to repay them.

The Seastone Keep golem crossed the line an easy first, followed by Raventor's solid, granite golem. Mistead's long strides brought it in third.

With the points all taken, all we had to do was finish. The GPS managed to gather a run for the last section, as Amy collapsed to the floor as though spent. It was a little over-dramatic, and the pig was still happily grunting, so it was all a little discordant, but I was impressed with her commitment. They just beat Sentraal's golem, narrowly avoiding last place.

With the race over, the golems were directed back to their camps, while the winning three protectorates were each presented with a beautiful token engraved with their points – someone in the village had clearly spent a lot of time making them.

Both our golem and Amy headed for the barn. It stopped in clear view of the main field so the exchange of teams through the golem's foot could take place. It shuddered slightly, but no other outward sign was visible. The transition took a few minutes, and after Amy had appeared to check the golem for damage, she returned with it to the main gate sentry position on the road.

My feet ached from standing still so long, and at some point, I'd gripped Royce's hand.

'Thanks,' he said as I released it. 'You have quite the grip, you know. Do you think we're getting away with it?'

I shrugged. Mistead had gathered by the lone tree in the field, their heads close together, and more than once, they glanced over at the barn. It was possible they thought we'd still had Lola's magic, or that they didn't know Fern was back, but I was certain they knew they had Amy's pig. We needed to be vigilant for them trying to expose us. With Amy's competition over, she needed to be careful.

Beth and a group of her staff pushed the gate open, dragging three huge metal objects behind them, then moved to a clear space, while some of the team set blankets on the grass. They opened the first lid as Satu joined them, with Dusty at her heels. She flourished her hands above the now open fire-cooker, and it burst into flames.

'How did she do that?' I whispered.

Royce pointed at a grinning Aran. 'I suspect he's been teaching her some tricks.'

Beth opened containers, placing coated meats and vegetables on the fire-cookers as Satu lit another. 'Please get comfortable. We would like you to indulge in a smoky taste and seasoning that we have been working on in honour of this Games.'

While the protectorates of the southern region mingled and chatted, spread around the field, those of Raventor and Mistead remained apart.

Seastone Keep's protectorate refused to take up the offer of the blankets to rest on and, in short order, had a luxurious seating arrangement laid out. They were last to eat, having spent their time getting suitably comfortable, and unwilling to fetch their own food.

'I always forget how obnoxiously entitled they are, living on that island,' Milla muttered between mouthfuls of food. 'It reminds me how much I like our quiet village. Even Amy is a joy compared to their attitude.'

I spotted movement at the edge of the woods from the corner of my eye. 'There's someone over there!' I whispered.

'Leave it to me,' Royce said. 'I need to feed the goats anyway. Have you got Doug?'

I pulled Doug into a cuddle, offering a belly rub and ear scratch as Royce called over to some of Aran's pole flight team. 'I could use a hand to get the animals fed. Don't want to miss out on anything.'

A couple of them grabbed their food and, as though some pre-arranged code had been triggered, joined him to walk toward the farm.

Chapter Twenty-Two

R oyce wasn't back. We'd finished lunch, and the bell for the start of the second session had rung from the roof of Pigs Might Fly.

As the staff of Phoenix Feather packed away the remnants of lunch and dragged things back to the inn, it started to rain.

At this time of year, that wasn't exactly unexpected, but rain would show up our spider silk threads for what they were. Even if the spectators couldn't see them, the nearest of the other teams would. Cari Elphic started walking across the field to the fencepost race. A magpie called from the wood – her own started to flutter and caw in response, a most unfamiliar-like behaviour. She strolled with a relaxed pace; no hesitation or tension visible from here, just her hand reaching up to soothe the bird. It did not appear to help.

The cow-eyed boy took up position next to her.

They were too far away now to hear any interactions, but as he put his arm out, a large hawk flew in to land on it. Even Milla's friendship spell might not withstand the magpie's instinct for self-preservation.

On the far side of the field, Aran's flag team was in position.

Purple flag. Cari took the magpie from her shoulder and sat it on the pole. I hoped Aran's hand sleight lessons had worked for her too.

All the other competitors stood their familiars next to or on their posts.

The green flag rose ... and fell.

The hawk took off, hovering high in the air as the fencepost lifted from the ground. Deep in the woods, I thought I saw movement again. A magpie called. Cari's magpie took off, and the post lifted – barely off the ground, but it counted. It tried to fly forward, but slowed as though being restrained. The post needed to move; the team needed to ease it, or we would be exposed. It tugged again, and straining with each wingbeat, began to fly toward its mate, who sat in the woods opposite Cari.

I realised at that point why Royce hadn't returned. Finding the mate in the trap again was a temptation hard to resist, although it was a bold test of Milla's spell.

The hawk above shrieked, swooping low as Mistead's fence-post shot across the field. Cari's magpie panicked, turning and biting at its foot.

Another low pass by the hawk as it flew to hover over the Mistead post was enough to break the charm. Cari's magpie struggled free of the tether and flew at full speed for the edge of the woods, its mate, and freedom. Our post followed, pulled no doubt by some of the villagers, trying to maintain the pretence.

My heart pounded. We were undone. Even if the post made it, the magpie wasn't coming back. We might have the mate, but Milla was nowhere near the wood, nor was Cari.

Mistead's post had reached the wood, and the hawk hovered above it as he changed its direction. Once again, the post took flight, speeding back to the start line. Ours turned ponderously, but the magpie didn't reappear. Without the familiar, the fencepost shouldn't fly.

From deep in the wood, a magpie soared skyward, swooping low as it skimmed the trees. Cari's head snapped up toward the bird, and she raised her hand, whistling loudly. Ralph swooped toward her, alighting on her shoulder and pecking at her ear. She reached for him and then sent him back up into the air. Ralph shrieked at the hawk, then flew directly to the post. A moment later, it lifted, flying almost as high as the trees back toward Cari.

I stroked Doug to hide the shaking of my hand. If Ralph was back, Gail had found the rest of them. Now, we just had to hold things in place until she returned. It wouldn't be before the Games were over, but with Ralph, Fern, and Dandelion in the village, we had a much better chance. If only pigs really could fly!

With my attention on the situation at the far side of the field, I'd missed who won the race and had to wait for the medals to be handed out. Raventor and Seastone Keep took the top spots again, with Chasmdeep coming in third.

At the speed Mistead had moved their post when they weren't attacking the poor magpie, they could have won. It was now apparent that our exposure was more important than their pride. We needed to keep our eyes on them.

The agitation on Cow-eyed Boy's face was far from hidden as he rejoined his protectorate. I watched as unobtrusively as I could to see his next move. He searched the crowd until he found Milla, who, for some reason, held a rabbit that – even to my eyes –wasn't Fern. He smiled at her with a predatory grin.

He thought he had us. Even if we had one familiar back, they would expect that we could be exposed or exploited. I still didn't truly understand their intent or motive, but we weren't giving up our village.

Crowds drifted away to their camps to regroup before the dazzling spectacle of fire-flight that evening.

It made sense to take Doug further from scrutiny to keep us from being exposed. As Royce hadn't yet returned, I called Doug to heel and headed toward the farm. Royce waved as we approached. He was caked in mud and sat outside, enjoying the last of the evening light.

'I made us some food,' he called as Doug ran to him, wagging so hard that it looked as though he'd fly better than Cari's fencepost.

I flopped into the other chair. Some sort of meaty scent drifted through the open door.

'That smells amazing, thank you.'

Royce took his glasses off to clean them on his shirt. It was one of the only bits of him that was clean. He saw me looking at his muddy trousers. 'Cuddles didn't like me leaving without his breakfast this morning, it turned out. He let me know in his own special way.'

It was good to see that he'd fallen foul of Cuddles too. He was caked, his boots tucked just outside the door as he wiggled his toes in striped socks.

'That post race was quite the moment. First rain, then the whole magpie flying off issue. Isn't it cheating for familiars to interfere the way that hawk did?'

I undid my own boots as I tried to work out what he'd cooked without asking. Whatever it was would be good – Royce had proven his talent there already.

'Technically, no. The hawk made no physical or magical contact. A true familiar wouldn't have been spooked by that behaviour. We'd have no grounds for complaint, and it might draw more attention to fake-Ralph's behaviour than we want.'

He put his glasses back on as he stood up. 'I'll go serve up our food. You can stay here.' He gestured for me to stay sitting as I moved to help him. 'You're my guest.' Royce paused, then looked away. 'You must be relieved that Ralph is back. If he's free, then it won't be long until Archie returns and you can move home.'

Without waiting for a reply, he vanished into the house to collect food. Royce was right. I couldn't wait to have Archie home, but the peace of this farm, the pleasant company, Doug ... I may have only been here for about a week, but it felt a good place. I was content sat on this porch with Royce and Doug. I felt more like myself than I had since I'd been called to join the protectorate.

He returned to the front porch with Doug following, twin streams of drool hanging in viscous hope from his mouth.

'It's nothing fancy, but it will keep us fed.'

The slice of golden, flaky-pastry topped pie sat in front of me like a symbol of all that was good about this farm. Thick gravy oozed from the edges of my slice, carrying chunks of tender meat, cooked long enough that it almost fell off my fork. Its outwardly plain, undecorated simplicity, the complex herbs and other flavours that mingled on my palette as the pastry crunched, then almost melted. The gravy held a hint of bay, wine, and juniper. Something fruity too. The meat was strong, and I couldn't help the sigh of satisfaction as I swallowed it.

'Is it okay?' Royce looked anxious.

'More than okay – it's amazing.' It really was.

'I like having someone to cook for.' He smiled shyly over the rim of his glasses before tucking into his own food.

'We should go back over,' I said as I wiped the last of the gravy up with bread.

'We can watch from this side of the field, if you like?' Royce pointed at the gathering lights in the distance in Pigs Might Fly's field.

While Milla had been carrying around that other rabbit, this was the one event where we had all the magic we needed. Milla wouldn't begrudge me watching from here, surely.

'We could just watch from here?' I suggested.

Royce nodded slowly. 'You could both use some more practise of the routine outdoors. Maybe we should.' He collected our plates and slipped back inside, returning a few minutes later with the music player and some blankets. 'Let's enjoy the fire-flight first, then we'll dance.'

The warm drink he handed me was syrupy and almost as delicious as his pie. We sat under blankets in the cool evening breeze, watching the sky light up. Flashes and waves of brilliant colour undulated across the sky; glowing lights floated over the trees, gently spinning and changing shades. Dazzling rainbow explosions, showers of shimmering light. Then, as the competition came near to the end, a glowing golden rabbit hopped across the sky.

As the light show faded and the strains of music from the party drifted across the field, we put our own music on.

Tomorrow, Doug and I had to fake our bond in front of all these people, and with no treats or cheese, we needed to dance. Tonight, we danced together. Whirling on the porch in socks, with Doug barking happily and bellies full of delicious food and happiness.

Chapter Twenty-Three

Morning came too fast. I woke to Royce tapping gently at the door. He pushed it open, and although my blankets were up to my neck, he still averted his eyes.

'I made you and Doug breakfast. You can't dance on an empty stomach. I'm going to feed the goats, so I can get dressed in clean clothes – and stay that way today.'

He smiled. 'I should be with you. It would look poor of me to not support your first Games event.' He closed the door again, and I heard him leave the house.

On the table was a warm roll, the fresh bread filled with dried fruits. Not the things we grew in Witchgorn either, or even those from the woods, but the rare kind we occasionally were able to buy when someone went to Nevsern. Next to it was a steaming cup of tea and a heap of fresh fruit on a pile of pancakes. Royce really didn't want me going hungry. Doug's food was in his bowl on the counter. Twin puddles of drool at his feet, stringing from his mouth once again as I lifted it down. Archie was not as drooly as Doug, but this dog was so clever, I hoped we could pull off the deception. Realistically, Archie was too stiff to dance around like Doug.

With breakfast eaten and the goats fed, we prepared with one last run-through inside the house. I focused on the subtleties of every hand gesture and body motion, every weave through my legs. Doug had learned it so well that he was almost anticipating the next step. If he could do that without me reminding him, it would look even better.

The pressures would be very different in a group of other animals, all dancing at the same time and surrounded by magic.

'I'd like to stop by Pigs Might Fly first.' It might let me speak to the others, find out about the night before. A twinge of guilt niggled at me over the choice to watch from the farm, but I was only doing as I'd been told. Practise and practise some more.

'I'll wait out here, try to find a good spot to watch from. Aran wants me anyway.' Royce wandered off without a backward glance. He'd forgotten to lead me to the steps. I searched the grass, hunting for a flattened patch that might give away Pigs Might Fly's location, desperate not to be the reason things fell apart now. The entire field was flattened.

An arm linked through mine.

'Did you see my rabbit?' Milla was glowing.

'I did! All the way from Royce's house.'

She glanced around. 'You mean from home, don't you? Eva, I won! It was risky keeping her tucked away so Cari couldn't ask me to drain her further, but it was worth letting her rest. We have some points. It's up to you this morning to earn us some more.'

I wasn't sure points were in my plan. All I wanted was to do my best and look as though I was using magic in some way. Keep up the illusion.

'Mistead are confused, and potentially dangerous, today. Be

careful – also of the step! Can't have you falling up the stairs again, can we?'

Her gentle guidance had led me to the steps. I climbed them with confidence, letting her open the door to expose the coffee area inside. It was filled with members of various protectorates, one sending a flame letter through the fire to someone.

The woman's blue-toned skirt dragged on the floor, and her posture hid her age. She turned to reveal someone barely older than Milla. Her eyes widened as she saw us, and she tried to shuffle away from the fire.

Milla sat at the counter, her fingers hovering over the cake selection. 'Want one?'

'No, Royce made us a big breakfast. I'd like to see if Cari is upstairs, though.' I left her trying to choose between treats that I suspected her mother had baked that morning.

There was no one up in our meeting room, but it gave me a good view of the circle that Aran had roped off. It was a single large area with a stage in the middle. The music would be live then. I hadn't prepared for that.

Along the town entrance, the golem kept up its steady patrol. The teams must be more exhausted than I could imagine after four days on rotation. They weren't due to change until lunchtime, but the golem ponderously worked its way toward the shed, then stopped in the changeover position. More frequent visits to that same spot would start to arouse suspicion soon. With the ring roped off, Aran made a direct line for Amy.

'Is there any way I can help you?' Cari's silent entrance made me jump. Doug barked at her too.

'I'm sorry. I was trying not to disturb your focus. I antici-pate that you will do an excellent job – given you stayed away last night to practise.'

'Yes, Mistress Cari,' I replied, dropping back to the way I'd addressed her since I was young. 'Unless you can give the power of speech to Doug, I think we're as ready as we can be. Did you notice that the golem went back early? I'm not sure how much longer the GPS will be able to keep going.'

'Leave them to Aran. Your job is to dance. Is the dog going to stay by you throughout, even when you take his lead off?'

'I believe he will.'

'Then you had better go down there.' Cari gestured at the other competitors starting to enter the roped off area. 'Do us proud, and I might soften your punishment.'

I ducked under the rope with Doug close at my heels, his eyes on the hand I kept deep in my treat pocket. I was competing in the Games. Me, Eva Eclipse. My heart raced, and excitement bubbled inside me, tinged with sadness ... I wasn't doing it with Archie.

I didn't look at the others to begin with, focused only on ensuring Doug's attention remained on me. But eventually, I spotted Berta and her snake taking position to my right, and a black-clad Raventor protectorate on my other side. I couldn't see his familiar, which meant that maybe Doug wouldn't either.

Royce stood behind the rope opposite me. His glasses reflected the sunlight, his clothes as clean as I'd ever seen them, aside from legs wet with rain-soaked grass to his shins. He attracted mud and water like—'

The music started. Doug immediately sat, ready for my instruction. We made eye contact for a full five seconds, his attention now fully on me. Then, that dog performed the best I could have asked for. He walked on his hind legs, he span; he wove between my legs as I ran in a circle. My movement made us stand out more, rather than the still pose of the others.

I was involved in the dance with Doug. He span on the

spot, then as I ducked down, he jumped on my back, leaping off again, just to walk backwards around me. We ran apart and back, to the left and to the right. We jumped and span some more. We ran out of moves, and Doug nudged at my pocket for his reward. I slipped one into a closed hand and tried to pass it to him with a flourish. There were people on the stage now. I didn't want to look, so I just started the routine all over again. The music stopped, and I asked Doug to bow while I returned a bow in his direction. The crowd burst into applause, cheering from all around us. Doug ran to Royce, jumping into his arms as I released him.

Toby Dogwood patted me on the shoulder. 'An unconventional display, Eva, and a crowd favourite. Sadly, we aren't supposed to move as well. It should be all about them. I commend you for your effort, though. Maybe next year you should aim to remain still – that's if you want to win.'

He leant in close and whispered, 'More magic, less training. I know you were late to this, but your protectorate should have given you more guidance there. Bloody impressive, though, either way.'

On the stage, the blue-robed woman who we'd caught sending the message sneered down at me. Alongside her, a black-clad Raventor leant in to whisper to her.

Maybe I'd not done well enough after all. I'd gone too far.

Royce had a good view of the ring from his position, and desperate to avoid being told I'd messed up, I joined him instead of rejoining my protectorate.

'You were brilliant – both of you,' he said. I didn't let him know that Toby had seen through my performance.

With the dancing over, Lola walked around the field, as did a number of others, studying the ground to find a place to grow their beanstalks.

She let a few others pick their spots before scrambling over the fence to look in the longer grass of the field. Lola gave a satisfied nod, then climbed back over with a flourish that belied her age. It would have cost her. I knew she wasn't using any of Dandelion's scarce magic for her own health.

There were no rules saying that they had to grow the beanstalk in the competition space, only that they had to stand in it. She'd made her decision look very casual – I hoped it would be enough.

Lola took her seed from the selection tray, kissed it, then offered it to Dandelion. He stretched and then curled up at her feet. She crouched, talking to him. Around the field, other familiars carried their seeds to the spots chosen by competitors, then dropped them. Dandelion got up after some nudging and, to a ripple of laughter from the spectators, jumped over the fence, before dropping it in the long grass.

Lola shrugged, as though helpless about the situation. Her back was to the other competitors as she started to make the plant grow.

A bird's-eye view would have exposed the slight separation of the surface to allow the tip of Larent's beanstalk to appear. I could barely watch. If the bubbles didn't work, the stalk wouldn't grow. It was always possible to claim Dandelion had simply gone back to sleep, but after all the work Larent and Beth had put in, I really hoped it would work.

I forced myself to keep watching. Slowly, Lola raised her hands skyward, and all I could do was hope the tiny amount of magic they could sustain for the skyhook was enough. Dandelion merely had to help lift the spider silk thread over the skyhook. It would take far less magic than actually growing a beanstalk.

Our beanstalk began to grow. It caught the wind, swaying as Dandelion must have lifted the thread. Light caught it for a moment, illuminating a thin line leading skyward. There was nothing we could do to help Lola aside from watch. I held back panic, resisting the urge to look and see who'd noticed.

'That's not good,' muttered Royce.

A cloud passed across the sun, the thread immediately less visible. It didn't look like a natural motion, and as I looked up, it appeared to have stopped drifting.

Milla stood to the far side of the ring – she hadn't moved. I couldn't see Cari. None of the crowd was looking up; they all cheered the extravagant beanstalks growing in the ring.

In the window of Pigs Might Fly, a figure dropped their arms. I wasn't entirely sure if it was Cari or someone older and more stooped.

Our beanstalk rose, each leaf fluttering freely as it caught the breeze. As it grew still taller, flowers appeared from the sides. The gas must have reached a high enough pressure to push them out.

Larent's talent was truly amazing. Aran had been right to encourage us to put our faith in him. All around, other vines and stalks grew. Some thick and entwining on themselves, some more like ours – slender and delicate Dandelion yawned from Lola's arms, a sign that we wouldn't have long before our skyhook might lose its grip. The large entwined beanstalk exploded, grown too fat and too thick, covering others in juice. I wiped a piece of green goop from my dress as Doug chewed a bit that had landed nearby.

With the first failure, the contest was over. Our small, but still present beanstalk remained in the running, at least until I turned to look at the rest.

Sentraal's beanstalk was incredible. Given the talent of the protectorate, they should be growing forests to protect them rather than relying on Westwick's golem. Our beanstalk was beautiful, but far shorter than the others, the gas limit having been reached a while before the explosion of Chasmdeep's.

Somehow, through Dandelion's snoring, it remained upright. It wouldn't remain that way for long, though. Lola looked exhausted and pale when she turned to be judged, but she beamed at me and waved, gesturing up at her beanstalk with pride.

The final points would be awarded, and we'd almost made it through.

Chapter Twenty-Four

Bunting hung from the stage, and vines wrapped around it as all the villages combined to make a beautiful spot for the awarding of the annual trophy. Black flowers bloomed, with feathers as petals, and lights twinkled between them as each village tried to add the most impressive decorations.

This was not a competition, yet it always became one. Milla sat on the floor near the stage, her hands buried deep in Fern's fur as a very small rabbit made of light hopped around the perimeter of the stage. Cari and Toby appeared from Pigs Might Fly, talking quietly as they approached. They took the stage together. Toby carried the box of blocks that initiated the Games sequence and symbolised both the winners and the next to host.

We gathered as a protectorate. Satu and Amy joined us, carefully positioned in the centre.

'The GPS can't keep going much longer,' Amy whispered. 'They're exhausted. It's going to take us a week to heal them all after this.'

Royce sat with us, his hand resting on Doug, as Dotty-The-

Second snuffled at him. 'I can't get the interior hooks out very quickly, even if someone else could take over.'

'They'll do it themselves if anyone can run the golem,' Amy replied.

Lola nudged Milla. 'Time to step up.'

Milla nodded. 'I can run it.' She let the rabbit do a final circuit, then fade away.

Paulie hovered on the edge of the stage, looking in our direction. Amy nodded at him, and he turned and ran to the barn.

'They'll remove them now,' Amy said.

I begrudgingly admired her. For the last three days, she'd been pretending to run the golem almost solo, and she'd kept Dotty-The-Second under control. She looked exhausted, her usually immaculate clothes mucky at the hems and her nails bitten down. In comparison, I'd had an easy few days. Guilt tinged the relief from successfully hiding that we'd lost our familiars. We'd not have had to do any of this if I'd known how to prevent them from being stolen. It all felt as though things had gone too well.

On the stage, the leaders of each protectorate took their places.

'With twelve points, in third place, it is Mistead.'

Cora stepped forward and released a bolt of lightning down, rain falling to either side as she took central stage.

'Mistead accepts third, and in addition, claims the territory of Witchgorn as being under-protected.'

A collective intake of breath, then noise erupted. 'Milla,' I hissed, 'you'd better be ready.' She ran toward the shed.

Cari laughed. 'Shall we deal with your claim after we celebrate the success of our winners? This is their moment.'

Seastone Keep's leader looked thoughtful. A gesture sent one of their protectorate running back to Phoenix Feather, just as one of Raventor's group did the same. Toby passed Cari a slip of paper. She unfurled it and continued, as though nothing had happened.

'Seastone Keep is in second place with thirteen points. And in first place, and hosts of next year's Games, is Raventor.'

She waited patiently. A calm centre to an almost-here storm. As soon as the box was handed over, Raventor raised it high.

'Next year will be the hardest, most challenging Games yet. Only the strongest will win.'

I held back a sigh. They were always so melodramatic.

A duck landed on the top of Pigs Might Fly. A very familiar duck.

Amy squeaked. 'Dotty's back – I can feel her.'

She was right. The tingle of magic started to refill me. Somewhere very close were the rest of our familiars. I could see Pigs Might Fly. Even it started to get up and stretch its legs, as though to greet them. It was all I could do not to leap to my feet and run to find Archie. Until Gail had them all back in our reach, we needed to hold our nerves.

Cari looked up at the duck and smiled.

'Now, shall we resolve Mistead's claim?' She gestured to the stage, allowing Cora to take her place.

'I believe that they do not have a full complement of protectorate. That the use of Lola is to hide this fact, and that that woman is no true magiker.' She pointed at me.

'I do not know how they have powered their golem, but its frequent rests show a weakness and vulnerability. The people of this village deserve protection. We offer ourselves to provide it.'

Seastone Keep stepped forward up at that point. 'It is not your call to make this offer. As the leaders of all protectorates in the region, it is our role to extend our protection to them. They are, after all, closer to us than you by land.'

Gail and Leesa wandered into the field. She looked up at the stage, and the familiars by her side disappeared.

A fluffy heap of smelly happiness arrived in our midst moments later. Seeing the motion in our group, Gail closed her hand, and the invisibility spell dropped.

We sat with two pigs, two goats, two dogs, a sleeping cat, and, as Gail and Leesa joined us, a duck flew down from Pigs Might Fly. I buried my face in Archie's curly, but rather smelly, coat.

'You need a bath,' I fussed at him as he snuggled into me.

'Perfect timing.' Amy grinned.

'Do you have any idea how hard it is to make Dotty run?' Leesa flopped to the ground. 'It's exhausting'

Cari gestured to our protectorate. 'It would appear that rather than under-protected, we are rather over-strength.'

The golem thudded across the field, its eyes glowing, to loom over the stage. Seastone Keep's leader looked at us and then turned to face Cora.

'I am not entirely sure what's going on here, but despite some irregularities, I do not see a village in need of protection.'

The golem rumbled loudly, its hollow interior giving a depth and volume to its voice that I truly appreciated for the first time.

'But...'

'Nice boat sheds you have,' Gail called out. 'There might be one less now, though, I'm afraid. Some things just can't be helped.'

Toby bit his lip as Berta put her hand over her mouth, her eyes creased with laughter. Cora strode from the stage in a most inelegant manner, gathering the rest of her protectorate as she left the field.

Our golem followed.

With the ceremony over and a long journey ahead of most of the protectorates, they started to move back to their tents.

Cari and Toby joined us, with the other Southern protectorate leaders close behind.

'You did well,' Toby said. 'I'm not sure we could have pulled that off as well as you did. I almost missed it, but I've never seen Satu pass up dancing with Jerry. That was my biggest clue. Although, I'd love to know how you managed to get that beanstalk so tall.'

Lola reached out to hug him. 'Thank you for the cloud.'

'Wasn't about to let a bit of sunlight spoil Dandelion's last Game,' he mumbled, blushing.

Lola slipped her arm through his. 'Come and have a coffee with me, and I'll tell you all about it.'

'Sounds delightful. How did you keep the golem running? That's the one I really need to know.'

'Ahh, now that's the one secret I won't divulge.' Lola winked at us as they walked off to Pigs Might Fly.

Slowly, our protectorate headed back to their homes, leaving Royce and me with the two dogs and Dusty.

Archie and Doug circled, sniffing and greeting each other like old friends. Doug ran away and back, bowing to try to initiate play. 'Go on,' I said, and Archie joined in, running around the field almost like a puppy again.

'I suppose I should collect my things.'

Royce shrugged. 'There's no rush. Why don't you stay for

dinner? You could come over more often, maybe. It's been nice having you around.' He stared at the ground as he asked.

'I'd love to.' Tomorrow, I'd be sorting out my mess. There were spiders to evict from the inn, Pigs Might Fly needed a proper feed of magic, Elsie would want her toes treated, and no doubt Farmer Tomkin would want Dotty-The-Second's spot cleaned off. And, on top of all that, someone would have to remove Dusty's fake genitals.

Yes, an evening of relaxation, in my new favourite place, with someone I now realised was my favourite person – before I had to help fix the village – would be lovely.

Acknowledgments

If you enjoyed Unfamiliared, I'd love it if you considered leaving review to help-others find the Two Chasms. I had a lot of fun writing this novella.

I've always wanted to write something a little cosy, a little humorous, and a little kind. There were always going to be animals and magic. But, it's taken me a while to feel I had the skills to do it.

Unfamiliared was supposed to be a standalone – a one off bit of joy. Now, it's the first instalment in the Two Chasms novellas.

As ever, even a small book takes a village. So thank you to Alex, for being an epic critique partner, and always braving the first draft!

Rowena, Vinjii, and Julia Thank you for your support and feedback. You are the best group of beta readers I could ask for.

My family are always a wonderful support as are the many friends who let me throw ideas at them.

Thank you all. Welcome to the Two Chasms.